Edith W[illegible]on

Short Stories

First published 2020

Dux Publishing is an imprint of Dux Enterprises Limited.
Contact at: publishing@duxenterprises.com

ISBN: 978-1-911538-79-0

Contents

The Triumph of Night 5
The Dilettante 41
The Fullness Of Life 57
The Muse's Tragedy 75
The Letters 95
The Pelican 133
The Pretext 161
Afterward 201
A Journey 247

The Triumph of Night

I

IT WAS CLEAR THAT THE SLEIGH FROM WEYMORE had not come; and the shivering young traveller from Boston, who had so confidently counted on jumping into it when he left the train at Northridge Junction, found himself standing alone on the open platform, exposed to the full assault of nightfall and winter.

The blast that swept him came off New Hampshire snow fields and ice-hung forests. It seemed to have traversed interminable leagues of frozen silence, filling them with the same cold roar and sharpening its edge against the same bitter black and white landscape. Dark, searching, and sword-like, it alternately muffled and harried its victim, like a bullfighter now whirling his cloak and now planting his darts. This analogy brought home to the young man the fact that he himself had no cloak, and that the overcoat in which he had faced the relatively temperate airs of Boston seemed no thicker than a sheet of paper on the bleak heights of Northridge. George Faxon said to himself that the place was uncommonly well named. It clung to an exposed ledge over the valley from which the train had lifted him, and the wind combed it with teeth of steel that he seemed actually to hear scraping against the wooden sides of the station. Other building there was none: the village lay far down the road, and thither—since the Weymore sleigh had not come—Faxon saw himself under the immediate necessity of plodding through several feet of snow.

He understood well enough what had happened at Weymore: his hostess had forgotten that he was coming. Young as Faxon was, this sad lucidity of soul had been acquired as the result of long experience, and he knew that the visitors who can least afford to hire a carriage are almost always those whom their hosts forget to send for. Yet to say Mrs. Culme had forgotten him was perhaps too crude a way of putting it. Similar incidents led him to think that she had probably told her maid to tell the butler to telephone the coachman to tell one of the grooms (if no one else needed him) to drive over to Northridge to fetch the new secretary; but on a night like this what groom who respected his rights would fail to forget the order?

Faxon's obvious course was to struggle through the drifts to the village, and there rout out a sleigh to convey him to Weymore; but what if, on his arrival at Mrs. Culme's, no one remembered to ask him what this devotion to duty had cost? That, again, was one of the contingencies he had expensively learned to look out for, and the perspicacity so acquired told him it would be cheaper to spend the night at the Northridge inn, and advise Mrs. Culme of his presence there by telephone. He had reached this decision, and was about to entrust his luggage to a vague man with a lantern who seemed to have some loose connection with the railway company, when his hopes were raised by the sound of sleigh bells.

Two vehicles were just dashing up to the station, and from the foremost there sprang a young man swathed in furs.

"Weymore?—No, these are not the Weymore sleighs."

The voice was that of the youth who had jumped to the platform—a voice so agreeable that, in spite of the words, it fell reassuringly on Faxon's ears. At the same moment the wandering station-lantern, casting a transient light on the speaker, showed his features to be in the pleasantest harmony with his voice. He was very fair and very young—hardly in the twenties, Faxon thought—but his face, though full of a morning freshness, was a trifle too thin and fine-drawn, as though a vivid spirit contended in him with a strain of physical weakness. Faxon was perhaps the quicker to notice such delicacies of balance because his own temperament hung on lightly vibrating nerves, which yet, as he believed, would never quite swing him beyond the arc of a normal sensibility.

"You expected a sleigh from Weymore?" the youth continued, standing beside Faxon like a slender column of fur.

Mrs. Culme's secretary explained his difficulty, and the newcomer brushed it aside with a contemptuous "Oh, Mrs. Culme!" that carried both speakers a long way toward reciprocal understanding.

"But then you must be—" The youth broke off with a smile of interrogation.

"The new secretary? Yes. But apparently there are no notes to be answered this evening." Faxon's laugh deepened the sense of solidarity which had so promptly established itself between the two.

The newcomer laughed also. "Mrs. Culme," he explained, "was lunching at my uncle's today, and she said you were due this evening. But seven hours is a long time for Mrs. Culme to remember anything."

"Well," said Faxon philosophically, "I suppose that's one of the reasons why she needs a secretary. And I've always the inn at Northridge," he concluded.

The youth laughed again. He was at the age when predicaments are food for gaiety.

"Oh, but you haven't, though! It burned down last week."

"The deuce it did!" said Faxon; but the humor of the situation struck him also before its inconvenience. His life, for years past, had been mainly a succession of resigned adaptations, and he had learned, before dealing practically with his embarrassments, to extract from most of them a small tribute of amusement.

"Oh, well, there's sure to be somebody in the place who can put me up."

"No one you could put up with. Besides, Northridge is three miles off, and our place—in the opposite direction—is a little nearer." Through the darkness, Faxon saw his friend sketch a gesture of self-introduction. "My name's Frank Rainer, and I'm staying with my uncle at Overdale. I've driven over to meet two friends of his, who are due in a few minutes from New York. If you don't mind waiting till they arrive I'm sure Overdale can do you better than Northridge. We're only down from town for a few days, but the house is always ready for a lot of people."

"But your uncle—?" Faxon could only object, with the odd sense, through his embarrassment, that it would be magically dispelled by his invisible friend's next words.

"Oh, my uncle—you'll see! I answer for HIM! I dare say you've heard of him—John Lavington?"

John Lavington! There was a certain irony in asking if one had heard of John Lavington! Even from a post of observation as obscure as that of Mrs. Culme's secretary, the rumor of John Lavington's money, of his pictures, his politics, his charities and his hospitality, was as difficult to escape as the roar of a cataract in a mountain solitude. It might almost have been said that the one place in which one would not have expected to come upon him was in just such a solitude as now surrounded the speakers—at least in this deepest hour of its desertedness. But it was just like Lavington's brilliant ubiquity to put one in the wrong even there.

"Oh, yes, I've heard of your uncle."

"Then you WILL come, won't you? We've only five minutes to wait," young Rainer urged, in the tone that dispels scruples by ignoring them; and Faxon found himself accepting the invitation as simply as it was offered.

A delay in the arrival of the New York train lengthened their five minutes to fifteen; and as they paced the icy platform Faxon began to see why it had seemed the most natural thing in the world to accede to his new acquaintance's suggestion. It was because Frank Rainer was one of the privileged beings who simplify human intercourse by the atmosphere of confidence and good humor they diffuse. He produced this effect, Faxon noted, by the exercise of no gift save his youth, of no art save his sincerity; but these qualities were revealed in a smile of such appealing sweetness that Faxon felt, as never before, what Nature can achieve when she deigns to match the face with the mind.

He learned that the young man was the ward, and only nephew, of John Lavington, with whom he had made his home since the death of his mother, the great man's sister. Mr. Lavington, Rainer said, had been "a regular brick" to him—"But then he is to every one, you know"—and the young fellow's situation seemed in fact to be perfectly in keeping with his person. Apparently the only shade that had ever rested on him was cast by the physical weakness which Faxon had already detected. Young Rainer had been threatened with a disease of the lungs which, according to the highest authorities, made banishment to Arizona or New Mexico inevitable. "But luckily my uncle didn't pack me off, as most people would have done, without getting another opinion. Whose? Oh, an awfully clever chap, a young doctor with a lot of new ideas, who simply laughed at my being sent away, and said I'd do perfectly well in New York if I didn't dine out too much, and if I dashed off occasionally to Northridge for a little fresh air. So it's really my uncle's doing that I'm not in exile—and I feel no end better since the new chap told me I needn't bother." Young Rainer went on to confess that he was extremely fond of dining out, dancing, and other urban distractions; and Faxon, listening to him, concluded that the physician who had refused to cut him off altogether from these pleasures was probably a better psychologist than his seniors.

"All the same you ought to be careful, you know." The sense of elder brotherly concern that forced the words from Faxon made him, as he spoke, slip his arm impulsively through Frank Rainer's.

The latter met the movement with a responsive pressure. "Oh, I AM: awfully, awfully. And then my uncle has such an eye on me!"

"But if your uncle has such an eye on you, what does he say to your swallowing knives out here in this Siberian wild?"

Rainer raised his fur collar with a careless gesture. "It's not that that does it—the cold's good for me."

"And it's not the dinners and dances? What is it, then?" Faxon good-humoredly insisted; to which his companion answered with a laugh: "Well, my uncle says it's being bored; and I rather think he's right!"

His laugh ended in a spasm of coughing and a struggle for breath that made Faxon, still holding his arm, guide him hastily into the shelter of the fireless waiting room.

Young Rainer had dropped down on the bench against the wall and pulled off one of his fur gloves to grope for a handkerchief. He tossed aside his cap and drew the handkerchief across his forehead, which was intensely white, and beaded with moisture, though his face retained a healthy glow. But Faxon's gaze remained fastened to the hand he had uncovered: it was so long, so colorless, so wasted, so much older than the brow he passed it over.

"It's queer—a healthy face but dying hands," the secretary mused; he somehow wished young Rainer had kept on his glove.

The whistle of the express drew the young men to their feet, and the next moment two heavily furred gentlemen had descended to the platform and were breasting the rigor of the night. Frank Rainer introduced them as Mr. Grisben and Mr. Balch, and Faxon, while their luggage was being lifted into the second sleigh, discerned them, by the roving lantern gleam, to be an elderly gray-headed pair, apparently of the average prosperous business cut.

They saluted their host's nephew with friendly familiarity, and Mr. Grisben, who seemed the spokesman of the two, ended his greeting with a genial—"and many many more of them, dear boy!" which suggested to Faxon that their arrival coincided with an anniversary. But he could not press the inquiry, for the seat allotted him was at the coachman's side, while Frank Rainer joined his uncle's guests inside the sleigh.

A swift flight (behind such horses as one could be sure of John Lavington's having) brought them to tall gateposts, an illuminated lodge, and an avenue on which the snow had been levelled to the smoothness of marble. At the end of the avenue the long house loomed through trees, its principal bulk dark but one wing sending out a ray of welcome; and the next moment Faxon was receiving a violent impression of warmth and light, of hothouse plants, hurrying servants, a vast spectacular oak hall like a stage setting, and, in its unreal middle distance, a small concise figure, correctly dressed, conventionally featured, and utterly unlike his rather florid conception of the great John Lavington.

The shock of the contrast remained with him through his hurried dressing in the large impersonally luxurious bedroom to which he had been shown. "I don't see where he comes in," was the only way he could put it, so difficult was it to fit the exuberance of Lavington's public personality into his host's contracted frame and manner. Mr. Lavington, to whom Faxon's case had been rapidly explained by young Rainer, had welcomed him with a sort of dry and stilted cordiality that exactly matched his narrow face, his stiff hand, the whiff of scent on his evening handkerchief. "Make yourself at home—at home!" he had repeated, in a tone that suggested, on his own part, a complete inability to perform the feat he urged on his visitor. "Any friend of Frank's … delighted … make yourself thoroughly at home!"

II

In spite of the balmy temperature and complicated conveniences of Faxon's bedroom, the injunction was not easy to obey. It was wonderful luck to have found a night's shelter under the opulent roof of Overdale, and he tasted the physical satisfaction to the full. But the place, for all its ingenuities of comfort, was oddly cold and unwelcoming. He couldn't have said why, and could only suppose that Mr. Lavington's intense personality—intensely negative, but intense all the same—must, in some occult way, have penetrated every corner of his dwelling. Perhaps, though, it was merely that Faxon himself was tired and hungry, more deeply chilled than he had known till he came in from the cold, and unutterably sick of all strange houses, and of the prospect of perpetually treading other people's stairs.

"I hope you're not famished?" Rainer's slim figure was in the doorway. "My uncle has a little business to attend to with Mr. Grisben, and we don't dine for half an hour. Shall I fetch you, or can you find your way down? Come straight to the dining room—the second door on the left of the long gallery."

He disappeared, leaving a ray of warmth behind him, and Faxon, relieved, lit a cigarette and sat down by the fire.

Looking about with less haste, he was struck by a detail that had escaped him. The room was full of flowers—a mere "bachelor's room," in the wing of a house opened only for a few days, in the dead middle of a New Hampshire winter! Flowers were everywhere, not in senseless profusion, but placed with the same conscious art he had remarked in the grouping of the blossoming shrubs that filled the hall. A vase of arums stood on the writing table, a cluster of strange-hued carnations on the stand at his elbow, and from wide bowls of glass and porcelain clumps of freesia bulbs diffused their melting fragrance. The fact implied acres of glass —but that was the least interesting part of it. The flowers themselves, their quality, selection and arrangement, attested on some one's part—and on whose but John Lavington's?—a solicitous and sensitive passion for that particular embodiment of beauty. Well, it simply made the man, as he had appeared to Faxon, all the harder to understand!

The half-hour elapsed, and Faxon, rejoicing at the near prospect of food, set out to make his way to the dining room. He had not noticed the direction he had followed in going to his room, and was puzzled, when he left it, to find that two staircases, of apparently equal importance, invited him. He chose the one to his right, and reached, at its foot, a long gallery such as Rainer had described. The gallery was empty, the doors down its length were closed; but Rainer had said: "The second to the left," and Faxon, after pausing for some chance enlightenment which did not come, laid his hand on the second knob to the left.

The room he entered was square, with dusky picture-hung

walls. In its centre, about a table lit by veiled lamps, he fancied Mr. Lavington and his guests to be already seated at dinner; then he perceived that the table was covered not with viands but with papers, and that he had blundered into what seemed to be his host's study. As he paused in the irresolution of embarrassment Frank Rainer looked up.

"Oh, here's Mr. Faxon. Why not ask him—?"

Mr. Lavington, from the end of the table, reflected his nephew's smile in a glance of impartial benevolence.

"Certainly. Come in, Mr. Faxon. If you won't think it a liberty—"

Mr. Grisben, who sat opposite his host, turned his solid head toward the door. "Of course Mr. Faxon's an American citizen?"

Frank Rainer laughed. "That all right! ... Oh, no, not one of your pin-pointed pens, Uncle Jack! Haven't you got a quill somewhere?"

Mr. Balch, who spoke slowly and as if reluctantly, in a muffled voice of which there seemed to be very little left, raised his hand to say: "One moment: you acknowledge this to be—?"

"My last will and testament?" Rainer's laugh redoubled. "Well, I won't answer for the 'last.' It's the first one, anyway."

"It's a mere formula," Mr. Balch explained.

"Well, here goes." Rainer dipped his quill in the inkstand

his uncle had pushed in his direction, and dashed a gallant signature across the document.

Faxon, understanding what was expected of him, and conjecturing that the young man was signing his will on the attainment of his majority, had placed himself behind Mr. Grisben, and stood awaiting his turn to affix his name to the instrument. Rainer, having signed, was about to push the paper across the table to Mr. Balch; but the latter, again raising his hand, said in his sad imprisoned voice: "The seal—?"

"Oh, does there have to be a seal?"

Faxon, looking over Mr. Grisben at John Lavington, saw a faint frown between his impassive eyes. "Really, Frank!" He seemed, Faxon thought, slightly irritated by his nephew's frivolity.

"Who's got a seal?" Frank Rainer continued, glancing about the table. "There doesn't seem to be one here."

Mr. Grisben interposed. "A wafer will do. Lavington, you have a wafer?"

Mr. Lavington had recovered his serenity. "There must be some in one of the drawers. But I'm ashamed to say I don't know where my secretary keeps these things. He ought, of course, to have seen to it that a wafer was sent with the document."

"Oh, hang it—" Frank Rainer pushed the paper aside: "It's the hand of God—and I'm hungry as a wolf. Let's dine first, Uncle Jack."

"I think I've a seal upstairs," said Faxon suddenly.

Mr. Lavington sent him a barely perceptible smile. "So sorry to give you the trouble—"

"Oh, I say, don't send him after it now. Let's wait till after dinner!"

Mr. Lavington continued to smile on his guest, and the latter, as if under the faint coercion of the smile, turned from the room and ran upstairs. Having taken the seal from his writing-case he came down again, and once more opened the door of the study. No one was speaking when he entered—they were evidently awaiting his return with the mute impatience of hunger, and he put the seal in Rainer's reach, and stood watching while Mr. Grisben struck a match and held it to one of the candles flanking the inkstand. As the wax descended on the paper Faxon remarked again the singular emaciation, the premature physical weariness, of the hand that held it: he wondered if Mr. Lavington had ever noticed his nephew's hand, and if it were not poignantly visible to him now.

With this thought in his mind, Faxon raised his eyes to look at Mr. Lavington. The great man's gaze rested on Frank Rainer with an expression of untroubled benevolence; and at the same instant Faxon's attention was attracted by the presence in the room of another person, who must have joined the group while he was upstairs searching for the seal. The new-comer was a man of about Mr. Lavington's age and figure, who stood directly behind his chair, and who, at the moment when Faxon first saw him, was gazing at young Rainer with an equal intensity of attention. The likeness between the two men—perhaps increased by the fact that the hooded lamps on the table left the figure behind the chair in shadow— struck Faxon the more because of the strange contrast in their expression. John Lavington, during his nephew's blundering attempt to drop the wax and apply the seal, continued to fasten on him a look of half-amused affection; while the man behind the chair, so oddly reduplicating the lines of his features and figure, turned on the boy a face of pale hostility.

The impression was so startling Faxon forgot what was going on about him. He was just dimly aware of young Rainer's exclaiming: "Your turn, Mr. Grisben!" of Mr. Grisben's ceremoniously protesting: "No—no; Mr. Faxon first," and of the pen's being thereupon transferred to his own hand. He received it with a deadly sense of being unable to move, or even to understand what was expected of him, till he became conscious of Mr. Grisben's paternally pointing out the precise spot on which he was to leave his autograph. The effort to fix his attention and steady his hand prolonged the process of signing, and when he stood up—a strange weight of fatigue on all his limbs—the figure behind Mr. Lavington's chair was gone.

Faxon felt an immediate sense of relief. It was puzzling that the man's exit should have been so rapid and noiseless, but the door behind Mr. Lavington was screened by a tapestry hanging, and Faxon concluded that the unknown looker-on had merely had to raise it to pass out. At any rate, he was gone, and with his withdrawal the strange weight was lifted. Young Rainer was lighting a cigarette, Mr. Balch meticulously inscribing his name at the foot of the document, Mr. Lavington—his eyes no longer on his nephew— examining a strange white-winged orchid in the vase at his elbow. Everything suddenly seemed to have grown natural and simple again, and Faxon found himself responding with a smile to the affable gesture with which his host declared: "And now, Mr. Faxon, we'll dine."

III

"I wonder how I blundered into the wrong room just now; I thought you told me to take the second door to the left," Faxon said to Frank Rainer as they followed the older men down the gallery.

"So I did; but I probably forgot to tell you which staircase to take. Coming from your bedroom, I ought to have said the fourth door to the right. It's a puzzling house, because my uncle keeps adding to it from year to year. He built this room last summer for his modern pictures."

Young Rainer, pausing to open another door, touched an electric button which sent a circle of light about the walls of a long room hung with canvases of the French impressionist school.

Faxon advanced, attracted by a shimmering Monet, but Rainer laid a hand on his arm.

"He bought that last week for a thundering price. But come along— I'll show you all this after dinner. Or HE will rather—he loves it."

"Does he really love things?"

Rainer stared, clearly perplexed at the question. "Rather!

Flowers and pictures especially! Haven't you noticed the flowers? I suppose you think his manner's cold; it seems so at first; but he's really awfully keen about things."

Faxon looked quickly at the speaker. "Has your uncle a brother?"

"Brother? No—never had. He and my mother were the only ones."

"Or any relation who—who looks like him? Who might be mistaken for him?"

"Not that I ever heard of. Does he remind you of some one?"

"Yes."

"That's queer. We'll ask him if he's got a double. Come on!"

But another picture had arrested Faxon, and some minutes elapsed before he and his young host reached the dining-room. It was a large room, with the same conventionally handsome furniture and delicately grouped flowers; and Faxon's first glance showed him that only three men were seated about the dining-table. The man who had stood behind Mr. Lavington's chair was not present, and no seat awaited him.

When the young men entered, Mr. Grisben was speaking, and his host, who faced the door, sat looking down at his untouched soup- plate and turning the spoon about in his small dry hand.

"It's pretty late to call them rumors—they were devilish close to facts when we left town this morning," Mr. Grisben was saying, with an unexpected incisiveness of tone.

Mr. Lavington laid down his spoon and smiled interrogatively. "Oh, facts—what are facts! Just the way a thing happens to look at a given minute."

"You haven't heard anything from town?" Mr. Grisben persisted.

"Not a syllable. So you see … Balch, a little more of that petite marmite. Mr. Faxon … between Frank and Mr. Grisben, please."

The dinner progressed through a series of complicated courses, ceremoniously dispensed by a stout butler attended by three tall footmen, and it was evident that Mr. Lavington took a somewhat puerile satisfaction in the pageant. That, Faxon reflected, was probably the joint in his armor—that and the flowers. He had changed the subject—not abruptly but firmly—when the young men entered, but Faxon perceived that it still possessed the thoughts of the two elderly visitors, and Mr. Balch presently observed, in a voice that seemed to come from the last survivor down a mine- shaft: "If it does come, it will be the biggest crash since '93."

Mr. Lavington looked bored but polite. "Wall Street can stand crashes better than it could then. It's got a robuster constitution."

"Yes; but—"

"Speaking of constitutions," Mr. Grisben intervened: "Frank, are you taking care of yourself?"

A flush rose to young Rainer's cheeks.

"Why, of course! Isn't that what I'm here for?"

"You're here about three days in the month, aren't you? And the rest of the time it's crowded restaurants and hot ballrooms in town. I thought you were to be shipped off to New Mexico?"

"Oh, I've got a new man who says that's rot."

"Well, you don't look as if your new man were right," said Mr. Grisben bluntly. Faxon saw the lad's color fade, and the rings of shadow deepen under his gay eyes. At the same moment his uncle turned to him with a renewed intensity of attention. There was such solicitude in Mr. Lavington's gaze that it seemed almost to fling a tangible shield between his nephew and Mr. Grisben's tactless scrutiny.

"We think Frank's a good deal better," he began; "this new doctor—"

The butler, coming up, bent discreetly to whisper a word in his ear, and the communication caused a sudden change in Mr. Lavington's expression. His face was naturally so colorless that it seemed not so much to pale as to fade, to dwindle and recede into something blurred and blotted-out. He half rose, sat down again and sent a rigid smile about the table.

"Will you excuse me? The telephone. Peters, go on with the dinner." With small precise steps he walked out of the door which one of the footmen had hastened to throw open.

A momentary silence fell on the group; then Mr. Grisben once more addressed himself to Rainer. "You ought to have gone, my boy; you ought to have gone."

The anxious look returned to the youth's eyes. "My uncle doesn't think so, really."

"You're not a baby, to be always governed on your uncle's opinion. You came of age to-day, didn't you? Your uncle spoils you … that's what's the matter…."

The thrust evidently went home, for Rainer laughed and looked down with a slight accession of color.

"But the doctor——"

"Use your common sense, Frank! You had to try twenty doctors to find one to tell you what you wanted to be told."

A look of apprehension overshadowed Rainer's gaiety. "Oh, come—I say! … What would YOU do?" he stammered.

"Pack up and jump on the first train." Mr. Grisben leaned forward and laid a firm hand on the young man's arm "Look here: my nephew Jim Grisben is out there ranching on a big scale. He'll take you in and be glad to have you. You say your new doctor thinks it won't do you any good; but he doesn't pretend to say it will do you harm, does he? Well, then—give it a trial. It'll take you out of hot theatres and night restaurants, anyhow…. And all the rest of it…. Eh, Balch?"

"Go!" said Mr. Balch hollowly. "Go AT ONCE," he added, as if a closer look at the youth's face had impressed on him the need of backing up his friend.

Young Rainer had turned ashy-pale. He tried to stiffen his mouth, into a smile. "Do I look as bad as all that?"

Mr. Grisben was helping himself to terrapin. "You look like the day after an earthquake," he said concisely.

The terrapin had encircled the table, and been deliberately enjoyed by Mr. Lavington's three visitors (Rainer, Faxon noticed, left his plate untouched) before the door was thrown open to re- admit their host.

Mr. Lavington advanced with an air of recovered composure. He seated himself, picked up his napkin, and consulted the gold- monogrammed menu. "No, don't bring back the filet.... Some terrapin; yes...." He looked affably about the table. "Sorry to have deserted you, but the storm has played the deuce with the wires, and I had to wait a long time before I could get a good connection. It must be blowing up for a blizzard."

"Uncle Jack," young Rainer broke out, "Mr. Grisben's been lecturing me."

Mr. Lavington was helping himself to terrapin. "Ah—what about?"

"He thinks I ought to have given New Mexico a show."

"I want him to go straight out to my nephew at Santa Paz and stay there till his next birthday." Mr. Lavington signed to the butler to hand the terrapin to Mr. Grisben, who, as he took a second helping, addressed himself again to Rainer. "Jim's in New York now, and going back the day after to-morrow in Olyphant's private car. I'll ask Olyphant to squeeze you in if you'll go. And when you've been out there a week or two, in the saddle all day and sleeping nine hours a night, I suspect you won't think much of the doctor who prescribed New York."

Faxon spoke up, he knew not why. "I was out there once: it's a splendid life. I saw a fellow—oh, a really BAD case—who'd been simply made over by it."

"It DOES sound jolly," Rainer laughed, a sudden eagerness of anticipation in his tone.

His uncle looked at him gently. "Perhaps Grisben's right. It's an opportunity——"

Faxon looked up with a start: the figure dimly perceived in the study was now more visibly and tangibly planted behind Mr. Lavington's chair.

"That's right, Frank: you see your uncle approves. And the trip out there with Olyphant isn't a thing to be missed. So drop a few dozen dinners and be at the Grand Central the day after to-morrow at five."

Mr. Grisben's pleasant gray eye sought corroboration of his host, and Faxon, in a cold anguish of suspense, continued to watch him as he turned his glance on Mr. Lavington. One could not look at Lavington without seeing the presence at his back, and it was clear that, the next minute, some change in Mr. Grisben's expression must give his watcher a clue.

But Mr. Grisben's expression did not change: the gaze he fixed on his host remained unperturbed, and the clue he gave was the startling one of not seeming to see the other figure.

Faxon's first impulse was to look away, to look anywhere else, to resort again to the champagne glass the watchful butler had already brimmed; but some fatal attraction, at war in him with an overwhelming physical resistance, held his eyes upon the spot they feared.

The figure was still standing, more distinctly, and therefore more resemblingly, at Mr. Lavington's back; and while the latter continued to gaze affectionately at his nephew, his counterpart, as before, fixed young Rainer with eyes of deadly menace.

Faxon, with what felt like an actual wrench of the muscles, dragged his own eyes from the sight to scan the other countenances about the table; but not one revealed the least consciousness of what he saw, and a sense of mortal isolation sank upon him.

"It's worth considering, certainly——" he heard Mr. Lavington continue; and as Rainer's face lit up, the face behind his uncle's chair seemed to gather into its look all the fierce weariness of old unsatisfied hates. That was the thing that, as the minutes labored by, Faxon was becoming most conscious of. The watcher behind the chair was no longer merely malevolent: he had grown suddenly, unutterably tired. His hatred seemed to well up out of the very depths of balked effort and thwarted hopes, and the fact made him more pitiable, and yet more dire.

Faxon's look reverted to Mr. Lavington, as if to surprise in him a corresponding change. At first none was visible: his pinched smile was screwed to his blank face like a gas-light to a white-washed wall. Then the fixity of the smile became ominous: Faxon saw that its wearer was afraid to let it go. It was evident that Mr. Lavington was unutterably tired too, and the discovery sent a colder current through Faxon's veins. Looking down at his untouched plate, he caught the soliciting twinkle of the champagne glass; but the sight of the wine turned him sick.

"Well, we'll go into the details presently," he heard Mr. Lavington say, still on the question of his nephew's future. "Let's have a cigar first. No—not here, Peters." He turned his smile on Faxon. "When we've had coffee I want to show you my pictures."

"Oh, by the way, Uncle Jack—Mr. Faxon wants to know if you've got a double?"

"A double?" Mr. Lavington, still smiling, continued to address himself to his guest. "Not that I know of. Have you seen one, Mr. Faxon?"

Faxon thought: "My God, if I look up now they'll BOTH be looking at me!" To avoid raising his eyes he made as though to lift the glass to his lips; but his hand sank inert, and he looked up. Mr. Lavington's glance was politely bent on him, but with a loosening of the strain about his heart he saw that the figure behind the chair still kept its gaze on Rainer.

"Do you think you've seen my double, Mr. Faxon?"

Would the other face turn if he said yes? Faxon felt a dryness in his throat. "No," he answered.

"Ah? It's possible I've a dozen. I believe I'm extremely usual- looking," Mr. Lavington went on conversationally; and still the other face watched Rainer.

"It was … a mistake … a confusion of memory …" Faxon heard himself stammer. Mr. Lavington pushed back his chair, and as he did so Mr. Grisben suddenly leaned forward. "Lavington! What have we been thinking of? We haven't drunk Frank's health!"

Mr. Lavington reseated himself. "My dear boy! … Peters, another bottle. …" He turned to his nephew. "After such a sin of omission I don't presume to propose the toast myself … but Frank knows. … Go ahead, Grisben!"

The boy shone on his uncle. "No, no, Uncle Jack! Mr. Grisben won't mind. Nobody but YOU—to-day!"

The butler was replenishing the glasses. He filled Mr. Lavington's last, and Mr. Lavington put out his small hand to raise it. … As he did so, Faxon looked away.

"Well, then—All the good I've wished you in all the past years. … I put it into the prayer that the coming ones may be healthy and happy and many … and MANY, dear boy!"

Faxon saw the hands about him reach out for their glasses. Automatically, he made the same gesture. His eyes were still on the table, and he repeated to himself with a trembling vehemence: "I won't look up! I won't …. I won't …." His fingers clasped the stem of the glass, and raised it to the level of his lips. He saw the other hands making the same motion. He heard Mr. Grisben's genial "Hear! Hear!" and Mr. Balch's hollow echo. He said to himself, as the rim of the glass touched his lips: "I won't look up! I swear I won't!—" and he looked.

The glass was so full that it required an extraordinary effort to hold it there, brimming and suspended, during the awful interval before he could trust his hand to lower it again, untouched, to the table. It was this merciful preoccupation which saved him, kept him from crying out, from losing his hold, from slipping down into the bottomless blackness that gaped for him. As long as the problem of the glass engaged him he felt able to keep his seat, manage his muscles, fit unnoticeably into the group; but as the glass touched the table his last link with safety snapped. He stood up and dashed out of the room.

IV

In the gallery, the instinct of self-preservation helped him to turn back and sign to young Rainer not to follow. He stammered out something about a touch of dizziness, and joining them presently; and the boy waved an unsuspecting hand and drew back.

At the foot of the stairs Faxon ran against a servant. "I should like to telephone to Weymore," he said with dry lips.

"Sorry, sir; wires all down. We've been trying the last hour to get New York again for Mr. Lavington."

Faxon shot on to his room, burst into it, and bolted the door. The mild lamplight lay on furniture, flowers, books, in the ashes a log still glimmered. He dropped down on the sofa and hid his face. The room was utterly silent, the whole house was still: nothing about him gave a hint of what was going on, darkly and dumbly, in the horrible room he had flown from, and with the covering of his eyes oblivion and reassurance seemed to fall on him. But they fell for a moment only; then his lids opened again to the monstrous vision. There it was, stamped on his pupils, a part of him forever, an indelible horror burnt into his body and brain. But why into his—just his? Why had he alone been chosen to see what he had seen? What business was it of HIS, in God's name! Any one of the others, thus enlightened, might have exposed the horror and defeated it; but HE, the one weaponless and defenceless spectator, the one whom none of the others would believe or understand if he attempted to reveal what he knew—HE alone had been singled out as the victim of this atrocious initiation!

Suddenly he sat up, listening: he had heard a step on the stairs. Some one, no doubt, was coming to see how he was—to urge him, if he felt better, to go down and join the smokers. Cautiously he opened his door; yes, it was young Rainer's step. Faxon looked down the passage, remembered the other stairway and darted to it. All he wanted was to get out of the house. Not another instant would he breathe its abominable air! What business was it of HIS, in God's name?

He reached the opposite end of the lower gallery, and beyond it saw the hall by which, he had entered. It was empty, and on a long table he recognized his coat and cap among the furs of the other travellers. He got into his coat, unbolted the door, and plunged into the purifying night.

The darkness was deep, and the cold so intense that for an instant it stopped his breathing. Then he perceived that only a thin snow was falling, and resolutely set his face for flight. The trees along the avenue dimly marked his way as he hastened with long strides over the beaten snow. Gradually, while he walked, the tumult in his brain subsided. The impulse to fly still drove him forward, but he began to feel that he was flying from a terror of his own creating, and that the most urgent reason for escape was the need of hiding his state, of shunning other eyes' scrutiny till he should regain his balance.

He had spent the long hours in the train in fruitless broodings on a discouraging situation, and he remembered how his bitterness had turned to exasperation when he found that the Weymore sleigh was not awaiting him. It was absurd, of course; but, though he had joked with Rainer over Mrs. Culme's forgetfulness, to confess it had cost a pang. That was what his rootless life had brought him to: for lack of a personal stake in things his sensibility was at the mercy of such trivial accidents. ... Yes; that, and the cold and fatigue, the absence of hope and the haunting sense of starved aptitudes, all these had brought him to the perilous verge over which, once or twice before, his terrified brain had hung.

Why else, in the name of any imaginable logic, human or devilish, should he, a stranger, be singled out for this experience? What could it mean to him, how was he related to it, what bearing had it on his case? ... Unless, indeed, it was just because he was a stranger-a stranger everywhere—because he had no personal life, no warm strong screen of private egotisms to shield him from exposure, that he had developed this abnormal sensitiveness to the vicissitudes of others. The thought pulled him up with a shudder. No! Such a fate was too abominable; all that was strong and sound in him rejected it. A thousand times better regard himself as ill, disorganized, deluded, than as the predestined victim of such warnings!

He reached the gates and paused before the darkened lodge. The wind had risen and was sweeping the snow into his face in lacerating streamers. The cold had him in its grasp again, and he stood uncertain. Should he put his sanity to the test and go back? He turned and looked down the dark drive to the house. A single ray shone through the trees, evoking a picture of the lights, the flowers, the faces grouped about that fatal room. He turned and plunged out into the road.

He remembered that, about a mile from Overdale, the coachman had pointed out the road to Northridge; and he began to walk in that direction. Once in the road, he had the gale in his face, and the wet snow on his moustache and eyelashes instantly hardened to metal. The same metal seemed to be driving a million blades into his throat and lungs, but he pushed on, desperately determined, the vision of the warm room pursuing him.

The snow in the road was deep and uneven. He stumbled across ruts and sank into drifts, and the wind rose before him like a granite cliff. Now and then he stopped, gasping, as if an invisible hand had tightened an iron band about his body; then he started again, stiffening himself against the stealthy penetration of the cold. The snow continued to descend out of a pall of inscrutable darkness, and once or twice he paused, fearing he had missed the road to Northridge; but, seeing no sign of a turn, he ploughed on doggedly.

At last, feeling sure that he had walked for more than a mile, he halted and looked back. The act of turning brought immediate relief, first because it put his back to the wind, and then because, far down the road, it showed him the advancing gleam of a lantern. A sleigh was coming—a sleigh that might perhaps give him a lift to the village! Fortified by the hope, he began to walk back toward the light. It seemed to come forward very slowly, with unaccountable zigzags and waverings; and even when he was within a few yards of it he could catch no sound of sleigh-bells. Then the light paused and became stationary by the roadside, as though carried by a pedestrian who had stopped, exhausted by the cold. The thought made Faxon hasten on, and a moment later he was stooping over a motionless figure huddled against the snow-bank. The lantern had dropped from its bearer's hand, and Faxon, fearfully raising it, threw its light into the face of Frank Rainer.

"Rainer! What on earth are you doing here!"

The boy smiled back through his pallor. "What are YOU, I'd like to know?" he retorted; and, scrambling to his feet with a clutch on Faxon's arm, he added gaily: "Well, I've run you down, anyhow!"

Faxon stood confounded, his heart sinking. The lad's face was gray.

"What madness—" he began.

"Yes, it IS. What on earth did you do it for?"

"I? Do what? … Why, I … I was just taking a walk. … I often walk at night. …"

Frank Rainer burst into a laugh. "On such nights? Then you hadn't bolted!"

"Bolted?"

"Because I'd done something to offend you? My uncle thought you had."

Faxon grasped his arm. "Did your uncle send you after me?"

"Well, he gave me an awful rowing for not going up to your room with you when you said you were ill. And when we found you'd gone we were frightened—and he was awfully upset—so I said I'd catch you. … You're NOT ill, are you?"

"Ill? No. Never better." Faxon picked up the lantern. "Come; let's go back. It was awfully hot in that dining-room," he added.

"Yes; I hoped it was only that."

They trudged on in silence for a few minutes; then Faxon questioned: "You're not too done up?"

"Oh, no. It's a lot easier with the wind behind us."

"All right. Don't talk any more."

They pushed ahead, walking, in spite of the light that guided them, more slowly than Faxon had walked alone into the gale. The fact of his companion's stumbling against a drift gave him a pretext for saying: "Take hold of my arm," and Rainer, obeying, gasped out: "I'm blown!"

"So am I. Who wouldn't be?"

"What a dance you led me! If it hadn't been for one of the servants' happening to see you—"

"Yes: all right. And now, won't you kindly shut up?"

Rainer laughed and hung on him. "Oh, the cold doesn't hurt me. …"

For the first few minutes after Rainer had overtaken him, anxiety for the lad had been Faxon's only thought. But as each laboring step carried them nearer to the spot he had been fleeing, the reasons for his flight grew more ominous and more insistent. No, he was not ill; he was not distraught and deluded—he was the instrument singled out to warn and save; and here he was, irresistibly driven, dragging the victim back to his doom!

The intensity of the conviction had almost checked his steps. But what could he do or say? At all costs he must get Rainer out of the cold, into the house and into his bed. After that he would act.

The snow-fall was thickening, and as they reached a stretch of the road between open fields the wind took them at an angle, lashing their faces with barbed thongs. Rainer stopped to take breath, and Faxon felt the heavier pressure of his arm.

"When we get to the lodge, can't we telephone to the stable for a sleigh?"

"If they're not all asleep at the lodge."

"Oh, I'll manage. Don't talk!" Faxon ordered; and they plodded on. …

At length the lantern ray showed ruts that curved away from the road under tree-darkness.

Faxon's spirits rose. "There's the gate! We'll be there in five minutes."

As he spoke he caught, above the boundary hedge, the gleam of a light at the farther end of the dark avenue. It was the same light that had shone on the scene of which every detail was burnt into his brain; and he felt again its overpowering reality. No—he couldn't let the boy go back!

They were at the lodge at last, and Faxon was hammering on the door. He said to himself: "I'll get him inside first, and make them give him a hot drink. Then I'll see—I'll find an argument. …"

There was no answer to his knocking, and after an interval Rainer said: "Look here—we'd better go on."

"No!"

"I can, perfectly—"

"You sha'n't go to the house, I say!" Faxon furiously redoubled his blows, and at length steps sounded on the stairs. Rainer was leaning against the lintel, and as the door opened the light from the hall flashed on his pale face and fixed eyes. Faxon caught him by the arm and drew him in.

"It WAS cold out there," he sighed; and then, abruptly, as if invisible shears at a single stroke had cut every muscle in his body, he swerved, drooped on Faxon's arm, and seemed to sink into nothing at his feet.

The lodge-keeper and Faxon bent over him, and somehow, between them, lifted him into the kitchen and laid him on a sofa by the stove.

The lodge-keeper, stammering: "I'll ring up the house," dashed out of the room. But Faxon heard the words without heeding them: omens mattered nothing now, beside this woe fulfilled. He knelt down to undo the fur collar about Rainer's throat, and as he did so he felt a warm moisture on his hands. He held them up, and they were red. …

V

The palms threaded their endless line along the yellow river. The little steamer lay at the wharf, and George Faxon, sitting in the veranda of the wooden hotel, idly watched the coolies carrying the freight across the gang plank.

He had been looking at such scenes for two months. Nearly five had elapsed since he had descended from the train at Northridge and strained his eyes for the sleigh that was to take him to Weymore: Weymore, which he was never to behold! … Part of the interval— the first part—was still a great gray blur. Even now he could not be quite sure how he had got back to Boston, reached the house of a cousin, and been thence transferred to a quiet room looking out on snow under bare trees. He looked out a long time at the same scene, and finally one day a man he had known at Harvard came to see him and invited him to go out on a business trip to the Malay Peninsula.

"You've had a bad shake-up, and it'll do you no end of good to get away from things."

When the doctor came the next day it turned out that he knew of the plan and approved it. "You ought to be quiet for a year. Just loaf and look at the landscape," he advised.

Faxon felt the first faint stirrings of curiosity.

"What's been the matter with me, anyhow?"

"Well, over-work, I suppose. You must have been bottling up for a bad breakdown before you started for New Hampshire last December. And the shock of that poor boy's death did the rest."

Ah, yes—Rainer had died. He remembered. …

He started for the East, and gradually, by imperceptible degrees, life crept back into his weary bones and leaden brain. His friend was very considerate and forbearing, and they travelled slowly and talked little. At first Faxon had felt a great shrinking from whatever touched on familiar things. He seldom looked at a newspaper, he never opened a letter without a moment's contraction of the heart. It was not that he had any special cause for apprehension, but merely that a great trail of darkness lay on everything. He had looked too deep down into the abyss. … But little by little health and energy returned to him, and with them the common promptings of curiosity. He was beginning to wonder how the world was going, and when, presently, the hotel-keeper told him there were no letters for him in the steamer's mail-bag, he felt a distinct sense of disappointment. His friend had gone into the jungle on a long excursion, and he was lonely, unoccupied, and wholesomely bored. He got up and strolled into the stuffy reading- room.

There he found a game of dominoes, a mutilated picture-puzzle, some copies of Zion's Herald, and a pile of New York and London newspapers.

He began to glance through the papers, and was disappointed to find that they were less recent than he had hoped. Evidently the last numbers had been carried off by luckier travellers. He continued to turn them over, picking out the American ones first. These, as it happened, were the oldest: they dated back to December and January. To Faxon, however, they had all the flavor of novelty, since they covered the precise period during which he had virtually ceased to exist. It had never before occurred to him to wonder what had happened in the world during that interval of obliteration; but now he felt a sudden desire to know.

To prolong the pleasure, he began by sorting the papers chronologically, and as he found and spread out the earliest number, the date at the top of the page entered into his consciousness like a key slipping into a lock. It was the seventeenth of December: the date of the day after his arrival at Northridge. He glanced at the first page and read in blazing characters: "Reported Failure of Opal Cement Company. Lavington's Name Involved. Gigantic Exposure of Corruption Shakes Wall Street to Its Foundations."

He read on, and when he had finished the first paper he turned to the next. There was a gap of three days, but the Opal Cement "Investigation" still held the centre of the stage. From its complex revelations of greed and ruin his eye wandered to the death notices, and he read: "Rainer. Suddenly, at Northridge, New Hampshire, Francis John, only son of the late. ..."

His eyes clouded, and he dropped the newspaper and sat for a long time with his face in his hands. When he looked up again he noticed that his gesture had pushed the other papers from the table and scattered them on the floor at his feet. The uppermost lay spread out before him, and heavily his eyes began their search again. "John Lavington comes forward with plan for reconstructing Company. Offers to put in ten millions of his own—The proposal under consideration by the District Attorney."

Ten millions … ten millions of his own. But if John Lavington was ruined? … Faxon stood up with a cry. That was it, then—that was what the warning meant! And if he had not fled from it, dashed wildly away from it into the night, he might have broken the spell of iniquity, the powers of darkness might not have prevailed! He caught up the pile of newspapers and began to glance through each in turn for the headline: "Wills Admitted to Probate". In the last of all he found the paragraph he sought, and it stared up at him as if with Rainer's dying eyes.

That—THAT was what he had done! The powers of pity had singled him out to warn and save, and he had closed his ears to their call, had washed his hands of it, and fled. Washed his hands of it! That was the word. It caught him back to the dreadful moment in the lodge when, raising himself up from Rainer's side, he had looked at his hands and seen that they were red. …

The Dilettante

It was on an impulse hardly needing the arguments he found himself advancing in its favor, that Thursdale, on his way to the club, turned as usual into Mrs. Vervain's street.

The "as usual" was his own qualification of the act; a convenient way of bridging the interval -- in days and other sequences -- that lay between this visit and the last. It was characteristic of him that he instinctively excluded his call two days earlier, with Ruth Gaynor, from the list of his visits to Mrs. Vervain: the special conditions attending it had made it no more like a visit to Mrs. Vervain than an engraved dinner invitation is like a personal letter. Yet it was to talk over his call with Miss Gaynor that he was now returning to the scene of that episode; and it was because Mrs. Vervain could be trusted to handle the talking over as skilfully as the interview itself that, at her corner, he had felt the dilettante's irresistible craving to take a last look at a work of art that was passing out of his possession.

On the whole, he knew no one better fitted to deal with the unexpected than Mrs. Vervain. She excelled in the rare art of taking things for granted, and Thursdale felt a pardonable pride in the thought that she owed her excellence to his training. Early in his career Thursdale had made the mistake, at the outset of his acquaintance with a lady, of telling her that he loved her and exacting the same avowal in return.

The latter part of that episode had been like the long walk back from a picnic, when one has to carry all the crockery one has finished using: it was the last time Thursdale ever allowed himself to be encumbered with the debris of a feast. He thus incidentally learned that the privilege of loving her is one of the least favors that a charming woman can accord; and in seeking to avoid the pitfalls of sentiment he had developed a science of evasion in which the woman of the moment became a mere implement of the game. He owed a great deal of delicate enjoyment to the cultivation of this art. The perils from which it had been his refuge became naively harmless: was it possible that he who now took his easy way along the levels had once preferred to gasp on the raw heights of emotion? Youth is a high-colored season; but he had the satisfaction of feeling that he had entered earlier than most into that chiar'oscuro of sensation where every half-tone has its value.

As a promoter of this pleasure no one he had known was comparable to Mrs. Vervain. He had taught a good many women not to betray their feelings, but he had never before had such fine material to work in. She had been surprisingly crude when he first knew her; capable of making the most awkward inferences, of plunging through thin ice, of recklessly undressing her emotions; but she had acquired, under the discipline of his reticences and evasions, a skill almost equal to his own, and perhaps more remarkable in that it involved keeping time with any tune he played and reading at sight some uncommonly difficult passages.

It had taken Thursdale seven years to form this fine talent; but the result justified the effort. At the crucial moment she had been perfect: her way of greeting Miss Gaynor had made him regret that he had announced his engagement by letter. It was an evasion that confessed a difficulty; a deviation implying an obstacle, where, by common consent, it was agreed to see none; it betrayed, in short, a lack of confidence in the completeness of his method. It had been his pride never to put himself in a position which had to be quitted, as it were, by the back door; but here, as he perceived, the main portals would have opened for him of their own accord. All this, and much more, he read in the finished naturalness with which Mrs. Vervain had met Miss Gaynor. He had never seen a better piece of work: there was no over-eagerness, no suspicious warmth, above all (and this gave her art the grace of a natural quality) there were none of those damnable implications whereby a woman, in welcoming her friend's betrothed, may keep him on pins and needles while she laps the lady in complacency. So masterly a performance, indeed, hardly needed the offset of Miss Gaynor's door-step words -- "To be so kind to me, how she must have liked you!" -- though he caught himself wishing it lay within the bounds of fitness to transmit them, as a final tribute, to the one woman he knew who was unfailingly certain to enjoy a good thing. It was perhaps the one drawback to his new situation that it might develop good things which it would be impossible to hand on to Margaret Vervain.

The fact that he had made the mistake of underrating his friend's powers, the consciousness that his writing must have betrayed his distrust of her efficiency, seemed an added reason for turning down her street instead of going on to the club. He would show her that he knew how to value her; he would ask her to achieve with him a feat infinitely rarer and more delicate than the one he had appeared to avoid. Incidentally, he would also dispose of the interval of time before dinner: ever since he had seen Miss Gaynor off, an hour earlier, on her return journey to Buffalo, he had been wondering how he should put in the rest of the afternoon. It was absurd, how he missed the girl. . . . Yes, that was it; the desire to talk about her was, after all, at the bottom of his impulse to call on Mrs. Vervain! It was absurd, if you like -- but it was delightfully rejuvenating. He could recall the time when he had been afraid of being obvious: now he felt that this return to the primitive emotions might be as restorative as a holiday in the Canadian woods. And it was precisely by the girl's candor, her directness, her lack of complications, that he was taken. The sense that she might say something rash at any moment was positively exhilarating: if she had thrown her arms about him at the station he would not have given a thought to his crumpled dignity. It surprised Thursdale to find what freshness of heart he brought to the adventure; and though his sense of irony prevented his ascribing his intactness to any conscious purpose, he could but rejoice in the fact that his sentimental economies had left him such a large surplus to draw upon.

Mrs. Vervain was at home -- as usual. When one visits the cemetery one expects to find the angel on the tombstone, and it struck Thursdale as another proof of his friend's good taste that she had been in no undue haste to change her habits. The whole house appeared to count on his coming; the footman took his hat and overcoat as naturally as though there had been no lapse in his visits; and the drawing-room at once enveloped him in that atmosphere of tacit intelligence which Mrs. Vervain imparted to her very furniture.

It was a surprise that, in this general harmony of circumstances, Mrs. Vervain should herself sound the first false note.

"You?" she exclaimed; and the book she held slipped from her hand.

It was crude, certainly; unless it were a touch of the finest art. The difficulty of classifying it disturbed Thursdale's balance.

"Why not?" he said, restoring the book. "Isn't it my hour?" And as she made no answer, he added gently, "Unless it's some one else's?"

She laid the book aside and sank back into her chair. "Mine, merely," she said.

"I hope that doesn't mean that you're unwilling to share it?"

"With you? By no means. You're welcome to my last crust."

He looked at her reproachfully. "Do you call this the last?"

She smiled as he dropped into the seat across the hearth. "It's a way of giving it more flavor!"

He returned the smile. "A visit to you doesn't need such condiments."

She took this with just the right measure of retrospective amusement.

"Ah, but I want to put into this one a very special taste," she confessed.

Her smile was so confident, so reassuring, that it lulled him into the imprudence of saying, "Why should you want it to be different from what was always so perfectly right?"

She hesitated. "Doesn't the fact that it's the last constitute a difference?"

"The last -- my last visit to you?"

"Oh, metaphorically, I mean -- there's a break in the continuity."

Decidedly, she was pressing too hard: unlearning his arts already!

"I don't recognize it," he said. "Unless you make me --" he added, with a note that slightly stirred her attitude of languid attention.

She turned to him with grave eyes. "You recognize no difference whatever?"

"None -- except an added link in the chain."

"An added link?"

"In having one more thing to like you for -- your letting Miss Gaynor see why I had already so many." He flattered himself that this turn had taken the least hint of fatuity from the phrase.

Mrs. Vervain sank into her former easy pose. "Was it that you came for?" she asked, almost gaily.

"If it is necessary to have a reason -- that was one."

"To talk to me about Miss Gaynor?"

"To tell you how she talks about you."

"That will be very interesting -- especially if you have seen her since her second visit to me."

"Her second visit?" Thursdale pushed his chair back with a start and moved to another. "She came to see you again?"

"This morning, yes -- by appointment."

He continued to look at her blankly. "You sent for her?"

"I didn't have to -- she wrote and asked me last night. But no doubt you have seen her since."

Thursdale sat silent. He was trying to separate his words from his thoughts, but they still clung together inextricably. "I saw her off just now at the station."

"And she didn't tell you that she had been here again?"

"There was hardly time, I suppose -- there were people about --" he floundered.

"Ah, she'll write, then."

He regained his composure. "Of course she'll write: very often, I hope. You know I'm absurdly in love," he cried audaciously.

She tilted her head back, looking up at him as he leaned against the chimney-piece. He had leaned there so often that the attitude touched a pulse which set up a throbbing in her throat. "Oh, my poor Thursdale!" she murmured.

"I suppose it's rather ridiculous," he owned; and as she remained silent, he added, with a sudden break --"Or have you another reason for pitying me?"

Her answer was another question. "Have you been back to your rooms since you left her?"

"Since I left her at the station? I came straight here."

"Ah, yes -- you could: there was no reason --" Her words passed into a silent musing.

Thursdale moved nervously nearer. "You said you had something to tell me?"

"Perhaps I had better let her do so. There may be a letter at your rooms."

"A letter? What do you mean? A letter from her? What has happened?"

His paleness shook her, and she raised a hand of reassurance. "Nothing has happened -- perhaps that is just the worst of it. You always hated, you know," she added incoherently, "to have things happen: you never would let them."

"And now -- ?"

"Well, that was what she came here for: I supposed you had guessed. To know if anything had happened."

"Had happened?" He gazed at her slowly. "Between you and me?" he said with a rush of light.

The words were so much cruder than any that had ever passed between them that the color rose to her face; but she held his startled gaze.

"You know girls are not quite as unsophisticated as they used to be. Are you surprised that such an idea should occur to her?"

His own color answered hers: it was the only reply that came to him.

Mrs. Vervain went on, smoothly: "I supposed it might have struck you that there were times when we presented that appearance."

He made an impatient gesture. "A man's past is his own!"

"Perhaps -- it certainly never belongs to the woman who has shared it. But one learns such truths only by experience; and Miss Gaynor is naturally inexperienced."

"Of course -- but -- supposing her act a natural one -- " he floundered lamentably among his innuendoes -- "I still don't see -- how there was anything --"

"Anything to take hold of? There wasn't --"

"Well, then -- ?" escaped him, in crude satisfaction; but as she did not complete the sentence he went on with a faltering laugh: "She can hardly object to the existence of a mere friendship between us!"

"But she does," said Mrs. Vervain.

Thursdale stood perplexed. He had seen, on the previous day, no trace of jealousy or resentment in his betrothed: he could still hear the candid ring of the girl's praise of Mrs. Vervain. If she were such an abyss of insincerity as to dissemble distrust under such frankness, she must at least be more subtle than to bring her doubts to her rival for solution. The situation seemed one through which one could no longer move in a penumbra, and he let in a burst of light with the direct query: "Won't you explain what you mean?"

Mrs. Vervain sat silent, not provokingly, as though to prolong his distress, but as if, in the attenuated phraseology he had taught her, it was difficult to find words robust enough to meet his challenge. It was the first time he had ever asked her to explain anything; and she had lived so long in dread of offering elucidations which were not wanted, that she seemed unable to produce one on the spot.

At last she said slowly: "She came to find out if you were really free."

Thursdale colored again. "Free?" he stammered, with a sense of physical disgust at contact with such crassness.

"Yes -- if I had quite done with you." She smiled in recovered security. "It seems she likes clear outlines; she has a passion for definitions."

"Yes -- well?" he said, wincing at the echo of his own subtlety.

"Well -- and when I told her that you had never belonged to me, she wanted me to define my status -- to know exactly where I had stood all along."

Thursdale sat gazing at her intently; his hand was not yet on the clue. "And even when you had told her that --"

"Even when I had told her that I had had no status -- that I had never stood anywhere, in any sense she meant," said Mrs. Vervain, slowly -- "even then she wasn't satisfied, it seems."

He uttered an uneasy exclamation. "She didn't believe you, you mean?"

"I mean that she did believe me: too thoroughly."

"Well, then -- in God's name, what did she want?"

"Something more -- those were the words she used."

"Something more? Between -- between you and me? Is it a conundrum?" He laughed awkwardly.

"Girls are not what they were in my day; they are no longer forbidden to contemplate the relation of the sexes."

"So it seems!" he commented. "But since, in this case, there wasn't any --" he broke off, catching the dawn of a revelation in her gaze.

"That's just it. The unpardonable offence has been -- in our not offending."

He flung himself down despairingly. "I give it up! -- What did you tell her?" he burst out with sudden crudeness.

"The exact truth. If I had only known," she broke off with a beseeching tenderness, "won't you believe that I would still have lied for you?"

"Lied for me? Why on earth should you have lied for either of us?"

"To save you -- to hide you from her to the last! As I've hidden you from myself all these years!" She stood up with a sudden tragic import in her movement. "You believe me capable of that, don't you? If I had only guessed -- but I have never known a girl like her; she had the truth out of me with a spring."

"The truth that you and I had never --"

"Had never -- never in all these years! Oh, she knew why -- she measured us both in a flash. She didn't suspect me of having haggled with you -- her words pelted me like hail. 'He just took what he wanted -- sifted and sorted you to suit his taste. Burnt out the gold and left a heap of cinders. And you let him -- you let yourself be cut in bits' -- she mixed her metaphors a little -- 'be cut in bits, and used or discarded, while all the while every drop of blood in you belonged to him! But he's Shylock -- and you have bled to death of the pound of flesh he has cut out of you.' But she despises me the most, you know -- far the most --" Mrs. Vervain ended.

The words fell strangely on the scented stillness of the room: they seemed out of harmony with its setting of afternoon intimacy, the kind of intimacy on which at any moment, a visitor might intrude without perceptibly lowering the atmosphere. It was as though a grand opera-singer had strained the acoustics of a private music-room.

Thursdale stood up, facing his hostess. Half the room was between them, but they seemed to stare close at each other now that the veils of reticence and ambiguity had fallen.

His first words were characteristic. "She does despise me, then?" he exclaimed.

"She thinks the pound of flesh you took was a little too near the heart."

He was excessively pale. "Please tell me exactly what she said of me."

"She did not speak much of you: she is proud. But I gather that while she understands love or indifference, her eyes have never been opened to the many intermediate shades of feeling. At any rate, she expressed an unwillingness to be taken with reservations -- she thinks you would have loved her better if you had loved some one else first. The point of view is original -- she insists on a man with a past!"

"Oh, a past -- if she's serious -- I could rake up a past!" he said with a laugh.

"So I suggested: but she has her eyes on his particular portion of it. She insists on making it a test case. She wanted to know what you had done to me; and before I could guess her drift I blundered into telling her."

Thursdale drew a difficult breath. "I never supposed -- your revenge is complete," he said slowly.

He heard a little gasp in her throat. "My revenge? When I sent for you to warn you -- to save you from being surprised as I was surprised?"

"You're very good -- but it's rather late to talk of saving me." He held out his hand in the mechanical gesture of leave-taking.

"How you must care! -- for I never saw you so dull," was her answer. "Don't you see that it's not too late for me to help you?" And as he continued to stare, she brought out sublimely: "Take the rest -- in imagination! Let it at least be of that much use to you. Tell her I lied to her -- she's too ready to believe it! And so, after all, in a sense, I sha'n't have been wasted."

His stare hung on her, widening to a kind of wonder. She gave the look back brightly, unblushingly, as though the expedient were too simple to need oblique approaches. It was extraordinary how a few words had swept them from an atmosphere of the most complex dissimulations to this contact of naked souls.

It was not in Thursdale to expand with the pressure of fate; but something in him cracked with it, and the rift let in new light. He went up to his friend and took her hand.

"You would do it -- you would do it!"

She looked at him, smiling, but her hand shook.

"Good-by," he said, kissing it.

"Good-by? You are going -- ?"

"To get my letter."

"Your letter? The letter won't matter, if you will only do what I ask."

He returned her gaze. "I might, I suppose, without being out of character. Only, don't you see that if your plan helped me it could only harm her?"

"Harm her?"

"To sacrifice you wouldn't make me different. I shall go on being what I have always been -- sifting and sorting, as she calls it. Do you want my punishment to fall on her?"

She looked at him long and deeply. "Ah, if I had to choose between you -- !"

"You would let her take her chance? But I can't, you see. I must take my punishment alone."

She drew her hand away, sighing. "Oh, there will be no punishment for either of you."

"For either of us? There will be the reading of her letter for me."

She shook her head with a slight laugh. "There will be no letter."

Thursdale faced about from the threshold with fresh life in his look. "No letter? You don't mean --"

"I mean that she's been with you since I saw her -- she's seen you and heard your voice. If there is a letter, she has recalled it -- from the first station, by telegraph."

He turned back to the door, forcing an answer to her smile. "But in the mean while I shall have read it," he said.

The door closed on him, and she hid her eyes from the dreadful emptiness of the room.

The Fullness Of Life

I

FOR HOURS SHE HAD LAIN IN A KIND OF gentle torpor, not unlike that sweet lassitude which masters one in the hush of a midsummer noon, when the heat seems to have silenced the very birds and insects, and, lying sunk in the tasselled meadow-grasses, one looks up through a level roofing of maple-leaves at the vast shadowless, and unsuggestive blue. Now and then, at ever-lengthening intervals, a flash of pain darted through her, like the ripple of sheet-lightning across such a midsummer sky; but it was too transitory to shake her stupor, that calm, delicious, bottomless stupor into which she felt herself sinking more and more deeply, without a disturbing impulse of resistance, an effort of reattachment to the vanishing edges of consciousness.

The resistance, the effort, had known their hour of violence; but now they were at an end. Through her mind, long harried by grotesque visions, fragmentary images of the life that she was leaving, tormenting lines of verse, obstinate presentments of pictures once beheld, indistinct impressions of rivers, towers, and cupolas, gathered in the length of journeys half forgotten-through her mind there now only moved a few primal sensations of colorless well-being; a vague satisfaction in the thought that she had swallowed her noxious last draught of medicine . . . and that she should never again hear the creaking of her husband's boots -- those horrible boots -- and that no one would come to bother her about the next day's dinner . . . or the butcher's book. . . .

At last even these dim sensations spent themselves in the thickening obscurity which enveloped her; a dusk now filled with pale geometric roses, circling softly, interminably before her, now darkened to a uniform blue-blackness, the hue of a summer night without stars. And into this darkness she felt herself sinking, sinking, with the gentle sense of security of one upheld from beneath. Like a tepid tide it rose around her, gliding ever higher and higher, folding in its velvety embrace her relaxed and tired body, now submerging her breast and shoulders, now creeping gradually, with soft inexorableness, over her throat to her chin, to her ears, to her mouth. . . . Ah, now it was rising too high; the impulse to struggle was renewed;. . . her mouth was full;. . . she was choking. . . . Help!

"It is all over," said the nurse, drawing down the eyelids with official composure.

The clock struck three. They remembered it afterward. Someone opened the window and let in a blast of that strange, neutral air which walks the earth between darkness and dawn; someone else led the husband into another room. He walked vaguely, like a blind man, on his creaking boots.

II

She stood, as it seemed, on a threshold, yet no tangible gateway was in front of her. Only a wide vista of light, mild yet penetrating as the gathered glimmer of innumerable stars, expanded gradually before her eyes, in blissful contrast to the cavernous darkness from which she had of late emerged.

She stepped forward, not frightened, but hesitating, and as her eyes began to grow more familiar with the melting depths of light about her, she distinguished the outlines of a landscape, at first swimming in the opaline uncertainty of Shelley's vaporous creations, then gradually resolved into distincter shape -- the vast unrolling of a sunlit plain, aerial forms of mountains, and presently the silver crescent of a river in the valley, and a blue stencilling of trees along its curve -- something suggestive in its ineffable hue of an azure background of Leonardo's, strange, enchanting, mysterious, leading on the eye and the imagination into regions of fabulous delight. As she gazed, her heart beat with a soft and rapturous surprise; so exquisite a promise she read in the summons of that hyaline distance.

"And so death is not the end after all," in sheer gladness she heard herself exclaiming aloud. "I always knew that it couldn't be. I believed in Darwin, of course. I do still; but then Darwin himself said that he wasn't sure about the soul -- at least, I think he did -- and Wallace was a spiritualist; and then there was St. George Mivart --"

Her gaze lost itself in the ethereal remoteness of the mountains.

"How beautiful! How satisfying!" she murmured. "Perhaps now I shall really know what it is to live."

As she spoke she felt a sudden thickening of her heart-beats, and looking up she was aware that before her stood the Spirit of Life.

"Have you never really known what it is to live?" the Spirit of Life asked her.

"I have never known," she replied, "that fulness of life which we all feel ourselves capable of knowing; though my life has not been without scattered hints of it, like the scent of earth which comes to one sometimes far out at sea."

"And what do you call the fulness of life?" the Spirit asked again.

"Oh, I can't tell you, if you don't know," she said, almost reproachfully. "Many words are supposed to define it -- love and sympathy are those in commonest use, but I am not even sure that they are the right ones, and so few people really know what they mean."

"You were married," said the Spirit, "yet you did not find the fulness of life in your marriage?"

"Oh, dear, no," she replied, with an indulgent scorn, "my marriage was a very incomplete affair."

"And yet you were fond of your husband?"

"You have hit upon the exact word; I was fond of him, yes,

just as I was fond of my grandmother, and the house that I was born in, and my old nurse. Oh, I was fond of him, and we were counted a very happy couple. But I have sometimes thought that a woman's nature is like a great house full of rooms: there is the hall, through which everyone passes in going in and out; the drawingroom, where one receives formal visits; the sitting-room, where the members of the family come and go as they list; but beyond that, far beyond, are other rooms, the handles of whose doors perhaps are never turned; no one knows the way to them, no one knows whither they lead; and in the innermost room, the holy of holies, the soul sits alone and waits for a footstep that never comes."

"And your husband," asked the Spirit, after a pause, "never got beyond the family sitting-room?"

"Never," she returned, impatiently; "and the worst of it was that he was quite content to remain there. He thought it perfectly beautiful, and sometimes, when he was admiring its commonplace furniture, insignificant as the chairs and tables of a hotel parlor, I felt like crying out to him: 'Fool, will you never guess that close at hand are rooms full of treasures and wonders, such as the eye of man hath not seen, rooms that no step has crossed, but that might be yours to live in, could you but find the handle of the door?'"

"Then," the Spirit continued, "those moments of which you lately spoke, which seemed to come to you like scattered hints of the fulness of life, were not shared with your husband?"

"Oh, no -- never. He was different. His boots creaked,

and he always slammed the door when he went out, and he never read anything but railway novels and the sporting advertisements in the papers -- and -- and, in short, we never understood each other in the least."

"To what influence, then, did you owe those exquisite sensations?"

"I can hardly tell. Sometimes to the perfume of a flower; sometimes to a verse of Dante or of Shakespeare; sometimes to a picture or a sunset, or to one of those calm days at sea, when one seems to be lying in the hollow of a blue pearl; sometimes, but rarely, to a word spoken by someone who chanced to give utterance, at the right moment, to what I felt but could not express."

"Someone whom you loved?" asked the Spirit.

"I never loved anyone, in that way," she said, rather sadly, "nor was I thinking of any one person when I spoke, but of two or three who, by touching for an instant upon a certain chord of my being, had called forth a single note of that strange melody which seemed sleeping in my soul. It has seldom happened, however, that I have owed such feelings to people; and no one ever gave me a moment of such happiness as it was my lot to feel one evening in the Church of Or San Michele, in Florence."

"Tell me about it," said the Spirit.

"It was near sunset on a rainy spring afternoon in Easter week. The clouds had vanished, dispersed by a sudden wind, and as we entered the church the fiery panes of the high windows shone out like lamps through the dusk. A priest was at the high altar, his white cope a livid spot in the incense-laden obscurity, the light of the candles flickering up and down like fireflies about his head; a few people knelt near by. We stole behind them and sat down on a bench close to the tabernacle of Orcagna.

"Strange to say, though Florence was not new to me, I had never been in the church before; and in that magical light I saw for the first time the inlaid steps, the fluted columns, the sculptured bas-reliefs and canopy of the marvellous shrine. The marble, worn and mellowed by the subtle hand of time, took on an unspeakable rosy hue, suggestive in some remote way of the honeycolored columns of the Parthenon, but more mystic, more complex, a color not born of the sun's inveterate kiss, but made up of cryptal twilight, and the flame of candles upon martyrs' tombs, and gleams of sunset through symbolic panes of chrysoprase and ruby; such a light as illumines the missals in the library of Siena, or burns like a hidden fire through the Madonna of Gian Bellini in the Church of the Redeemer, at Venice; the light of the Middle Ages, richer, more solemn, more significant than the limpid sunshine of Greece.

"The church was silent, but for the wail of the priest and the occasional scraping of a chair against the floor, and as I sat there, bathed in that light, absorbed in rapt contemplation of the marble miracle which rose before me, cunningly wrought as a casket of ivory and enriched with jewel-like incrustations and tarnished gleams of gold, I felt myself borne onward along a mighty current, whose source seemed to be in the very beginning of things, and whose tremendous waters gathered as they went all the mingled streams of human passion and endeavor. Life in all its varied manifestations of beauty and strangeness seemed weaving a rhythmical dance around me as I moved, and wherever the spirit of man had passed I knew that my foot had once been familiar.

"As I gazed the mediaeval bosses of the tabernacle of Orcagna seemed to melt and flow into their primal forms so that the folded lotus of the Nile and the Greek acanthus were braided with the runic knots and fish-tailed monsters of the North, and all the plastic terror and beauty born of man's hand from the Ganges to the Baltic quivered and mingled in Orcagna's apotheosis of Mary. And so the river bore me on, past the alien face of antique civilizations and the familiar wonders of Greece, till I swam upon the fiercely rushing tide of the Middle Ages, with its swirling eddies of passion, its heaven-reflecting pools of poetry and art; I heard the rhythmic blow of the craftsmen's hammers in the goldsmiths' workshops and on the walls of churches, the party-cries of armed factions in the narrow streets, the organroll of Dante's verse, the crackle of the fagots around Arnold of Brescia, the twitter of the swallows to which St. Francis preached, the laughter of the ladies listening on the hillside to the quips of the Decameron, while plague-struck Florence howled beneath them -- all this and much more I heard, joined in strange unison with voices earlier and more remote, fierce, passionate, or tender, yet subdued to such awful harmony that I thought of the song that the morning stars sang together and felt as though it were sounding in my ears. My heart beat to suffocation, the tears burned my lids, the joy, the mystery of it seemed too intolerable to be borne. I could not understand even then the words of the song; but I knew that if there had been someone at my side who could have heard it with me, we might have found the key to it together.

"I turned to my husband, who was sitting beside me in an attitude of patient dejection, gazing into the bottom of his hat; but at that moment he rose, and stretching his stiffened legs, said, mildly: 'Hadn't we better be going? There doesn't seem to be much to see here, and you know the table d'hote dinner is at half-past six o'clock."

Her recital ended, there was an interval of silence; then the Spirit of Life said: "There is a compensation in store for such needs as you have expressed."

"Oh, then you do understand?" she exclaimed. "Tell me what compensation, I entreat you!"

"It is ordained," the Spirit answered, "that every soul which seeks in vain on earth for a kindred soul to whom it can lay bare its inmost being shall find that soul here and be united to it for eternity."

A glad cry broke from her lips. "Ah, shall I find him at last?" she cried, exultant.

"He is here," said the Spirit of Life.

She looked up and saw that a man stood near whose soul (for in that unwonted light she seemed to see his soul more clearly than his face) drew her toward him with an invincible force.

"Are you really he?" she murmured.

"I am he," he answered.

She laid her hand in his and drew him toward the parapet which overhung the valley.

"Shall we go down together," she asked him, "into that marvellous country; shall we see it together, as if with the self-same eyes, and tell each other in the same words all that we think and feel?"

"So," he replied, "have I hoped and dreamed."

"What?" she asked, with rising joy. "Then you, too, have looked for me?"

"All my life."

"How wonderful! And did you never, never find anyone in the other world who understood you?"

"Not wholly -- not as you and I understand each other."

"Then you feel it, too? Oh, I am happy," she sighed.

They stood, hand in hand, looking down over the parapet upon the shimmering landscape which stretched forth beneath them into sapphirine space, and the Spirit of Life, who kept watch near the threshold, heard now and then a floating fragment of their talk blown backward like the stray swallows which the wind sometimes separates from their migratory tribe.

"Did you never feel at sunset --"

"Ah, yes; but I never heard anyone else say so. Did you?"

"Do you remember that line in the third canto of the 'Inferno?'"

"Ah, that line -- my favorite always. Is it possible --"

"You know the stooping Victory in the frieze of the Nike Apteros?"

"You mean the one who is tying her sandal? Then you have noticed, too, that all Botticelli and Mantegna are dormant in those flying folds of her drapery?"

"After a storm in autumn have you never seen --"

"Yes, it is curious how certain flowers suggest certain painters-the perfume of the incarnation, Leonardo; that of the rose, Titian; the tuberose, Crivelli --"

"I never supposed that anyone else had noticed it."

"Have you never thought --"

"Oh, yes, often and often; but I never dreamed that anyone else had."

"But surely you must have felt --"

"Oh, yes, yes; and you, too --"

"How beautiful! How strange --"

Their voices rose and fell, like the murmur of two fountains answering each other across a garden full of flowers. At length, with a certain tender impatience, he turned to her and said: “Love, why should we linger here? All eternity lies before us. Let us go down into that beautiful country together and make a home for ourselves on some blue hill above the shining river.”

As he spoke, the hand she had forgotten in his was suddenly withdrawn, and he felt that a cloud was passing over the radiance of her soul.

“A home,” she repeated, slowly, “a home for you and me to live in for all eternity?”

“Why not, love? Am I not the soul that yours has sought?”

“Y-yes -- yes, I know -- but, don’t you see, home would not be like home to me, unless --”

“Unless?” he wonderingly repeated.

She did not answer, but she thought to herself, with an impulse of whimsical inconsistency, “Unless you slammed the door and wore creaking boots.”

But he had recovered his hold upon her hand, and by imperceptible degrees was leading her toward the shining steps which descended to the valley.

“Come, O my soul’s soul,” he passionately implored; “why delay a moment? Surely you feel, as I do, that eternity itself is too short to hold such bliss as ours. It seems to me that I can see our home already. Have I not always seem it in my dreams? It is white, love, is it not, with polished columns, and a sculptured cornice against the blue? Groves of laurel and oleander and thickets of roses surround it; but from the terrace where we walk at sunset, the eye looks out over woodlands and cool meadows where, deep-bowered under ancient boughs, a stream goes delicately toward the river. Indoors our favorite pictures hang upon the walls and the rooms are lined with books. Think, dear, at last we shall have time to read them all. With which shall we begin? Come, help me to choose. Shall it be 'Faust' or the 'Vita Nuova,' the 'Tempest' or 'Les Caprices de Marianne,' or the thirty-first canto of the 'Paradise,' or 'Epipsychidion' or "Lycidas'? Tell me, dear, which one?"

As he spoke he saw the answer trembling joyously upon her lips; but it died in the ensuing silence, and she stood motionless, resisting the persuasion of his hand.

"What is it?" he entreated.

"Wait a moment," she said, with a strange hesitation in her voice. "Tell me first, are you quite sure of yourself? Is there no one on earth whom you sometimes remember?"

"Not since I have seen you," he replied; for, being a man, he had indeed forgotten.

Still she stood motionless, and he saw that the shadow deepened on her soul.

"Surely, love," he rebuked her, "it was not that which troubled you? For my part I have walked through Lethe. The past has melted like a cloud before the moon. I never lived until I saw you."

She made no answer to his pleadings, but at length, rousing herself with a visible effort, she turned away from him and moved toward the Spirit of Life, who still stood near the threshold.

"I want to ask you a question," she said, in a troubled voice.

"Ask," said the Spirit.

"A little while ago," she began, slowly, "you told me that every soul which has not found a kindred soul on earth is destined to find one here."

"And have you not found one?" asked the Spirit.

"Yes; but will it be so with my husband's soul also?"

"No," answered the Spirit of Life, "for your husband imagined that he had found his soul's mate on earth in you; and for such delusions eternity itself contains no cure."

She gave a little cry. Was it of disappointment or triumph?

"Then -- then what will happen to him when he comes here?"

"That I cannot tell you. Some field of activity and happiness he will doubtless find, in due measure to his capacity for being active and happy."

She interrupted, almost angrily: "He will never be happy without me."

"Do not be too sure of that," said the Spirit.

She took no notice of this, and the Spirit continued: "He will not understand you here any better than he did on earth."

"No matter," she said; "I shall be the only sufferer, for he always thought that he understood me."

"His boots will creak just as much as ever --"

"No matter."

"And he will slam the door --"

"Very likely."

"And continue to read railway novels --"

She interposed, impatiently: "Many men do worse than that."

"But you said just now," said the Spirit, "that you did not love him."

"True," she answered, simply; "but don't you understand that I shouldn't feel at home without him? It is all very well for a week or two -- but for eternity! After all, I never minded the creaking of his boots, except when my head ached, and I don't suppose it will ache here; and he was always so sorry when he had slammed the door, only he never could remember not to. Besides, no one else would know how to look after him, he is so helpless. His inkstand would never be filled, and he would always be out of stamps and visiting-cards. He would never remember to have his umbrella re-covered, or to ask the price of anything before he bought it. Why, he wouldn't even know what novels to read. I always had to choose the kind he liked, with a murder or a forgery and a successful detective."

She turned abruptly to her kindred soul, who stood listening with a mien of wonder and dismay.

"Don't you see," she said, "that I can't possibly go with you?"

"But what do you intend to do?" asked the Spirit of Life.

"What do I intend to do?" she returned, indignantly. "Why, I mean to wait for my husband, of course. If he had come here first he would have waited for me for years and years; and it would break his heart not to find me here when he comes." She pointed with a contemptuous gesture to the magic vision of hill and vale sloping away to the translucent mountains. "He wouldn't give a fig for all that," she said, "if he didn't find me here."

"But consider," warned the Spirit, "that you are now choosing for eternity. It is a solemn moment."

"Choosing!" she said, with a half-sad smile. "Do you still keep up here that old fiction about choosing? I should have thought that you knew better than that. How can I help myself? He will expect to find me here when he comes, and he would never believe you if you told him that I had gone away with someone else-never, never."

"So be it," said the Spirit. "Here, as on earth, each one must decide for himself."

She turned to her kindred soul and looked at him gently, almost wistfully. "I am sorry," she said. "I should have liked to talk with you again; but you will understand, I know, and I dare say you will find someone else a great deal cleverer --"

And without pausing to hear his answer she waved him a swift farewell and turned back toward the threshold.

"Will my husband come soon?" she asked the Spirit of Life.

"That you are not destined to know," the Spirit replied.

"No matter," she said, cheerfully; "I have all eternity to wait in."

And still seated alone on the threshold, she listens for the creaking of his boots.

The Muse's Tragedy

DANYERS AFTERWARDS LIKED TO FANCY that he had recognized Mrs. Anerton at once; but that, of course, was absurd, since he had seen no portrait of her--she affected a strict anonymity, refusing even her photograph to the most privileged--and from Mrs. Memorall, whom he revered and cultivated as her friend, he had extracted but the one impressionist phrase: "Oh, well, she's like one of those old prints where the lines have the value of color."

He was almost certain, at all events, that he had been thinking of Mrs. Anerton as he sat over his breakfast in the empty hotel restaurant, and that, looking up on the approach of the lady who seated herself at the table near the window, he had said to himself, "_That might be she_."

Ever since his Harvard days--he was still young enough to think of them as immensely remote--Danyers had dreamed of Mrs. Anerton, the Silvia of Vincent Rendle's immortal sonnet-cycle, the Mrs. A. of the _Life and Letters_. Her name was enshrined in some of the noblest English verse of the nineteenth century--and of all past or future centuries, as Danyers, from the stand-point of a maturer judgment, still believed. The first reading of certain poems--of the _ Antinous_, the _Pia Tolomei_, the _Sonnets to Silvia_,--had been epochs in Danyers's growth, and the verse seemed to gain in mellowness, in amplitude, in meaning as one brought to its interpretation more experience of life, a finer emotional sense. Where, in his boyhood, he had felt only the perfect, the almost austere beauty of form, the subtle interplay of vowel-sounds, the rush and fulness of lyric emotion, he now thrilled to the close-packed significance of each line, the allusiveness of each word--his imagination lured hither and thither on fresh trails of thought, and perpetually spurred by the sense that, beyond what he had already discovered, more marvellous regions lay waiting to be explored. Danyers had written, at college, the prize essay on Rendle's poetry (it chanced to be the moment of the great man's death); he had fashioned the fugitive verse of his own storm-and-stress period on the forms which Rendle had first given to English metre; and when two years later the _Life and Letters_ appeared, and the Silvia of the sonnets took substance as Mrs. A., he had included in his worship of Rendle the woman who had inspired not only such divine verse but such playful, tender, incomparable prose.

Danyers never forgot the day when Mrs. Memorall happened to mention that she knew Mrs. Anerton. He had known Mrs. Memorall for a year or more, and had somewhat contemptuously classified her as the kind of woman who runs cheap excursions to celebrities; when one afternoon she remarked, as she put a second lump of sugar in his tea:

"Is it right this time? You're almost as particular as Mary Anerton."

"Mary Anerton?"

"Yes, I never _can_ remember how she likes her tea. Either

it's lemon _with_ sugar, or lemon without sugar, or cream without either, and whichever it is must be put into the cup before the tea is poured in; and if one hasn't remembered, one must begin all over again. I suppose it was Vincent Rendle's way of taking his tea and has become a sacred rite."

"Do you _know_ Mrs. Anerton?" cried Danyers, disturbed by this careless familiarity with the habits of his divinity.

"'And did I once see Shelley plain?' Mercy, yes! She and I were at school together--she's an American, you know. We were at a _pension_ near Tours for nearly a year; then she went back to New York, and I didn't see her again till after her marriage. She and Anerton spent a winter in Rome while my husband was attached to our Legation there, and she used to be with us a great deal." Mrs. Memorall smiled reminiscently. "It was _the_ winter."

"The winter they first met?"

"Precisely--but unluckily I left Rome just before the meeting took place. Wasn't it too bad? I might have been in the _Life and Letters_. You know he mentions that stupid Madame Vodki, at whose house he first saw her."

"And did you see much of her after that?"

"Not during Rendle's life. You know she has lived in Europe almost entirely, and though I used to see her off and on when I went abroad, she was always so engrossed, so preoccupied, that one felt one wasn't wanted. The fact is, she cared only about his friends--she separated herself gradually from all her own people. Now, of course, it's different; she's desperately lonely; she's taken to writing to me now and then; and last year, when she heard I was going abroad, she asked me to meet her in Venice, and I spent a week with her there."

"And Rendle?"

Mrs. Memorall smiled and shook her head. "Oh, I never was allowed a peep at _him_; none of her old friends met him, except by accident. Ill-natured people say that was the reason she kept him so long. If one happened in while he was there, he was hustled into Anerton's study, and the husband mounted guard till the inopportune visitor had departed. Anerton, you know, was really much more ridiculous about it than his wife. Mary was too clever to lose her head, or at least to show she'd lost it--but Anerton couldn't conceal his pride in the conquest. I've seen Mary shiver when he spoke of Rendle as _our poet_. Rendle always had to have a certain seat at the dinner-table, away from the draught and not too near the fire, and a box of cigars that no one else was allowed to touch, and a writing-table of his own in Mary's sitting-room--and Anerton was always telling one of the great man's idiosyncrasies: how he never would cut the ends of his cigars, though Anerton himself had given him a gold cutter set with a star-sapphire, and how untidy his writing-table was, and how the house- maid had orders always to bring the waste-paper basket to her mistress before emptying it, lest some immortal verse should be thrown into the dust-bin."

"The Anertons never separated, did they?"

"Separated? Bless you, no. He never would have left Rendle! And besides, he was very fond of his wife."

"And she?"

"Oh, she saw he was the kind of man who was fated to make himself ridiculous, and she never interfered with his natural tendencies."

From Mrs. Memorall, Danyers further learned that Mrs. Anerton, whose husband had died some years before her poet, now divided her life between Rome, where she had a small apartment, and England, where she occasionally went to stay with those of her friends who had been Rendle's. She had been engaged, for some time after his death, in editing some juvenilia which he had bequeathed to her care; but that task being accomplished, she had been left without definite occupation, and Mrs. Memorall, on the occasion of their last meeting, had found her listless and out of spirits.

"She misses him too much--her life is too empty. I told her so--I told her she ought to marry."

"Oh!"

"Why not, pray? She's a young woman still--what many people would call young," Mrs. Memorall interjected, with a parenthetic glance at the mirror. "Why not accept the inevitable and begin over again? All the King's horses and all the King's men won't bring Rendle to life-and besides, she didn't marry _him_ when she had the chance."

Danyers winced slightly at this rude fingering of his idol. Was it possible that Mrs. Memorall did not see what an anti-climax such a marriage would have been? Fancy Rendle "making an honest woman" of Silvia; for so society would have viewed it! How such a reparation would have vulgarized their past--it would have been like "restoring" a masterpiece; and how exquisite must have been the perceptions of the woman who, in defiance of appearances, and perhaps of her own secret inclination, chose to go down to posterity as Silvia rather than as Mrs. Vincent Rendle!

Mrs. Memorall, from this day forth, acquired an interest in Danyers's eyes. She was like a volume of unindexed and discursive memoirs, through which he patiently plodded in the hope of finding embedded amid layers of dusty twaddle some precious allusion to the subject of his thought. When, some months later, he brought out his first slim volume, in which the remodelled college essay on Rendle figured among a dozen, somewhat overstudied "appreciations," he offered a copy to Mrs. Memorall; who surprised him, the next time they met, with the announcement that she had sent the book to Mrs. Anerton.

Mrs. Anerton in due time wrote to thank her friend. Danyers was privileged to read the few lines in which, in terms that suggested the habit of "acknowledging" similar tributes, she spoke of the author's "feeling and insight," and was "so glad of the opportunity," etc. He went away disappointed, without clearly knowing what else he had expected.

The following spring, when he went abroad, Mrs. Memorall offered him letters to everybody, from the Archbishop of Canterbury to Louise Michel. She did not include Mrs. Anerton, however, and Danyers knew, from a previous conversation, that Silvia objected to people who "brought letters." He knew also that she travelled during the summer, and was unlikely to return to Rome before the term of his holiday should be reached, and the hope of meeting her was not included among his anticipations.

The lady whose entrance broke upon his solitary repast in the restaurant of the Hotel Villa d'Este had seated herself in such a way that her profile was detached against the window; and thus viewed, her domed forehead, small arched nose, and fastidious lip suggested a silhouette of Marie Antoinette. In the lady's dress and movements--in the very turn of her wrist as she poured out her coffee--Danyers thought he detected the same fastidiousness, the same air of tacitly excluding the obvious and unexceptional. Here was a woman who had been much bored and keenly interested. The waiter brought her a _Secolo,_ and as she bent above it Danyers noticed that the hair rolled back from her forehead was turning gray; but her figure was straight and slender, and she had the invaluable gift of a girlish back.

The rush of Anglo-Saxon travel had not set toward the lakes, and with the exception of an Italian family or two, and a hump-backed youth with an _abbe_, Danyers and the lady had the marble halls of the Villa d'Este to themselves.

When he returned from his morning ramble among the hills he saw her sitting at one of the little tables at the edge of the lake. She was writing, and a heap of books and newspapers lay on the table at her side. That evening they met again in the garden. He had strolled out to smoke a last cigarette before dinner, and under the black vaulting of ilexes, near the steps leading down to the boat-landing, he found her leaning on the parapet above the lake. At the sound of his approach she turned and looked at him. She had thrown a black lace scarf over her head, and in this sombre setting her face seemed thin and unhappy. He remembered afterwards that her eyes, as they met his, expressed not so much sorrow as profound discontent.

To his surprise she stepped toward him with a detaining gesture.

"Mr. Lewis Danyers, I believe?"

He bowed.

"I am Mrs. Anerton. I saw your name on the visitors' list and wished to thank you for an essay on Mr. Rendle's poetry--or rather to tell you how much I appreciated it. The book was sent to me last winter by Mrs. Memorall."

She spoke in even melancholy tones, as though the habit of perfunctory utterance had robbed her voice of more spontaneous accents; but her smile was charming. They sat down on a stone bench under the ilexes, and she told him how much pleasure his essay had given her. She thought it the best in the book--she was sure he had put more of himself into it than into any other; was she not right in conjecturing that he had been very deeply influenced by Mr. Rendle's poetry? _Pour comprendre il faut aimer_, and it seemed to her that, in some ways, he had penetrated the poet's inner meaning more completely than any other critic. There were certain problems, of course, that he had left untouched; certain aspects of that many-sided mind that he had perhaps failed to seize--

"But then you are young," she concluded gently, "and one could not wish you, as yet, the experience that a fuller understanding would imply."

II

She stayed a month at Villa d'Este, and Danyers was with her daily. She showed an unaffected pleasure in his society; a pleasure so obviously founded on their common veneration of Rendle, that the young man could enjoy it without fear of fatuity. At first he was merely one more grain of frankincense on the altar of her insatiable divinity; but gradually a more personal note crept into their intercourse. If she still liked him only because he appreciated Rendle, she at least perceptibly distinguished him from the herd of Rendle's appreciators.

Her attitude toward the great man's memory struck Danyers as perfect. She neither proclaimed nor disavowed her identity. She was frankly Silvia to those who knew and cared; but there was no trace of the Egeria in her pose. She spoke often of Rendle's books, but seldom of himself; there was no posthumous conjugality, no use of the possessive tense, in her abounding reminiscences. Of the master's intellectual life, of his habits of thought and work, she never wearied of talking. She knew the history of each poem; by what scene or episode each image had been evoked; how many times the words in a certain line had been transposed; how long a certain adjective had been sought, and what had at last suggested it; she could even explain that one impenetrable line, the torment of critics, the joy of detractors, the last line of _The Old Odysseus_.

Danyers felt that in talking of these things she was no mere echo of Rendle's thought. If her identity had appeared to be merged in his it was because they thought alike, not because he had thought for her. Posterity is apt to regard the women whom poets have sung as chance pegs on which they hung their garlands; but Mrs. Anerton's mind was like some fertile garden wherein, inevitably, Rendle's imagination had rooted itself and flowered. Danyers began to see how many threads of his complex mental tissue the poet had owed to the blending of her temperament with his; in a certain sense Silvia had herself created the _Sonnets to Silvia_.

To be the custodian of Rendle's inner self, the door, as it were, to the sanctuary, had at first seemed to Danyers so comprehensive a privilege that he had the sense, as his friendship with Mrs. Anerton advanced, of forcing his way into a life already crowded. What room was there, among such towering memories, for so small an actuality as his? Quite suddenly, after this, he discovered that Mrs. Memorall knew better: his fortunate friend was bored as well as lonely.

"You have had more than any other woman!" he had exclaimed to her one day; and her smile flashed a derisive light on his blunder. Fool that he was, not to have seen that she had not had enough! That she was young still--do years count?--tender, human, a woman; that the living have need of the living.

After that, when they climbed the alleys of the hanging park, resting in one of the little ruined temples, or watching, through a ripple of foliage, the remote blue flash of the lake, they did not always talk of Rendle or of literature. She encouraged Danyers to speak of himself; to confide his ambitions to her; she asked him the questions which are the wise woman's substitute for advice.

"You must write," she said, administering the most exquisite flattery that human lips could give.

Of course he meant to write--why not to do something great in his turn? His best, at least; with the resolve, at the outset, that his best should be _the_ best. Nothing less seemed possible with that mandate in his ears. How she had divined him; lifted and disentangled his groping ambitions; laid the awakening touch on his spirit with her creative _Let there be light!_

It was his last day with her, and he was feeling very hopeless and happy.

"You ought to write a book about _him,"_ she went on gently.

Danyers started; he was beginning to dislike Rendle's way of walking in unannounced.

"You ought to do it," she insisted. "A complete interpretation--a summing- up of his style, his purpose, his theory of life and art. No one else could do it as well."

He sat looking at her perplexedly. Suddenly--dared he guess?

"I couldn't do it without you," he faltered.

"I could help you--I would help you, of course."

They sat silent, both looking at the lake.

It was agreed, when they parted, that he should rejoin her six weeks later in Venice. There they were to talk about the book.

III

Lago d'Iseo, August 14th.

When I said good-by to you yesterday I promised to come back to Venice in a week: I was to give you your answer then. I was not honest in saying that; I didn't mean to go back to Venice or to see you again. I was running away from you--and I mean to keep on running! If _you_ won't, _I_ must. Somebody must save you from marrying a disappointed woman of--well, you say years don't count, and why should they, after all, since you are not to marry me?

That is what I dare not go back to say. _You are not to marry me_. We have had our month together in Venice (such a good month, was it not?) and now you are to go home and write a book--any book but the one we--didn't talk of!--and I am to stay here, attitudinizing among my memories like a sort of female Tithonus. The dreariness of this enforced immortality!

But you shall know the truth. I care for you, or at least for your love, enough to owe you that.

You thought it was because Vincent Rendle had loved me that there was so little hope for you. I had had what I wanted to the full; wasn't that what you said? It is just when a man begins to think he understands a woman that he may be sure he doesn't! It is because Vincent Rendle _didn't love me_ that there is no hope for you. I never had what I wanted, and never, never, never will I stoop to wanting anything else.

Do you begin to understand? It was all a sham then, you

say? No, it was all real as far as it went. You are young--you haven't learned, as you will later, the thousand imperceptible signs by which one gropes one's way through the labyrinth of human nature; but didn't it strike you, sometimes, that I never told you any foolish little anecdotes about him? His trick, for instance, of twirling a paper-knife round and round between his thumb and forefinger while he talked; his mania for saving the backs of notes; his greediness for wild strawberries, the little pungent Alpine ones; his childish delight in acrobats and jugglers; his way of always calling me _you--dear you_, every letter began--I never told you a word of all that, did I? Do you suppose I could have helped telling you, if he had loved me? These little things would have been mine, then, a part of my life--of our life--they would have slipped out in spite of me (it's only your unhappy woman who is always reticent and dignified). But there never was any "our life;" it was always "our lives" to the end....

If you knew what a relief it is to tell some one at last, you would bear with me, you would let me hurt you! I shall never be quite so lonely again, now that some one knows.

Let me begin at the beginning. When I first met Vincent Rendle I was not twenty-five. That was twenty years ago. From that time until his death, five years ago, we were fast friends. He gave me fifteen years, perhaps the best fifteen years, of his life. The world, as you know, thinks that his greatest poems were written during those years; I am supposed to have "inspired" them, and in a sense I did. From the first, the intellectual sympathy between us was almost complete; my mind must have been to him (I fancy) like some perfectly tuned instrument on which he was never tired of playing. Some one told me of his once saying of me that I "always understood;" it is the only praise I ever heard of his giving me. I don't even know if he thought me pretty, though I hardly think my appearance could have been disagreeable to him, for he hated to be with ugly people. At all events he fell into the way of spending more and more of his time with me. He liked our house; our ways suited him. He was nervous, irritable; people bored him and yet he disliked solitude. He took sanctuary with us. When we travelled he went with us; in the winter he took rooms near us in Rome. In England or on the continent he was always with us for a good part of the year. In small ways I was able to help him in his work; he grew dependent on me. When we were apart he wrote to me continually--he liked to have me share in all he was doing or thinking; he was impatient for my criticism of every new book that interested him; I was a part of his intellectual life. The pity of it was that I wanted to be something more. I was a young woman and I was in love with him--not because he was Vincent Rendle, but just because he was himself!

People began to talk, of course--I was Vincent Rendle's Mrs. Anerton; when the _Sonnets to Silvia_ appeared, it was whispered that I was Silvia. Wherever he went, I was invited; people made up to me in the hope of getting to know him; when I was in London my doorbell never stopped ringing. Elderly peeresses, aspiring hostesses, love-sick girls and struggling authors overwhelmed me with their assiduities. I hugged my success, for I knew what it meant--they thought that Rendle was in love with me! Do you know, at times, they almost made me think so too? Oh, there was no phase of folly I didn't go through. You can't imagine the excuses a woman will invent for a man's not telling her that he loves her--pitiable arguments that she would see through at a glance if any other woman used them! But all the while, deep down,

I knew he had never cared. I should have known it if he had made love to me every day of his life. I could never guess whether he knew what people said about us--he listened so little to what people said; and cared still less, when he heard. He was always quite honest and straightforward with me; he treated me as one man treats another; and yet at times I felt he _must_ see that with me it was different. If he did see, he made no sign. Perhaps he never noticed--I am sure he never meant to be cruel. He had never made love to me; it was no fault of his if I wanted more than he could give me. The _Sonnets to Silvia_, you say? But what are they? A cosmic philosophy, not a love-poem; addressed to Woman, not to a woman!

But then, the letters? Ah, the letters! Well, I'll make a clean breast of it. You have noticed the breaks in the letters here and there, just as they seem to be on the point of growing a little--warmer? The critics, you may remember, praised the editor for his commendable delicacy and good taste (so rare in these days!) in omitting from the correspondence all personal allusions, all those _details intimes_ which should be kept sacred from the public gaze. They referred, of course, to the asterisks in the letters to Mrs. A. Those letters I myself prepared for publication; that is to say, I copied them out for the editor, and every now and then I put in a line of asterisks to make it appear that something had been left out. You understand? The asterisks were a sham--_there was nothing to leave out_.

No one but a woman could understand what I went through during those years--the moments of revolt, when I felt I must break away from it all, fling the truth in his face and never see him again; the inevitable reaction, when not to see him seemed the one unendurable thing, and I trembled lest a look or word of mine should disturb the poise of our friendship; the silly days when I hugged the delusion that he _must_ love me, since everybody thought he did; the long periods of numbness, when I didn't seem to care whether he loved me or not. Between these wretched days came others when our intellectual accord was so perfect that I forgot everything else in the joy of feeling myself lifted up on the wings of his thought. Sometimes, then, the heavens seemed to be opened....

* * * * *

All this time he was so dear a friend! He had the genius of friendship, and he spent it all on me. Yes, you were right when you said that I have had more than any other woman. _Il faut de l'adresse pour aimer_, Pascal says; and I was so quiet, so cheerful, so frankly affectionate with him, that in all those years I am almost sure I never bored him. Could I have hoped as much if he had loved me?

You mustn't think of him, though, as having been tied to my skirts. He came and went as he pleased, and so did his fancies. There was a girl once (I am telling you everything), a lovely being who called his poetry "deep" and gave him _Lucile_ on his birthday. He followed her to Switzerland one summer, and all the time that he was dangling after her (a little too conspicuously, I always thought, for a Great Man), he was writing to _me_ about his theory of vowel-combinations--or was it his experiments in English hexameter? The letters were dated from the very places where I knew they went and sat by waterfalls together and he thought out adjectives for her hair. He talked to me about it quite frankly afterwards.

She was perfectly beautiful and it had been a pure delight to watch her; but she _would_ talk, and her mind, he said, was "all elbows." And yet, the next year, when her marriage was announced, he went away alone, quite suddenly ... and it was just afterwards that he published _Love's Viaticum_. Men are queer!

After my husband died--I am putting things crudely, you see--I had a return of hope. It was because he loved me, I argued, that he had never spoken; because he had always hoped some day to make me his wife; because he wanted to spare me the "reproach." Rubbish! I knew well enough, in my heart of hearts, that my one chance lay in the force of habit. He had grown used to me; he was no longer young; he dreaded new people and new ways; _il avait pris son pli_. Would it not be easier to marry me?

I don't believe he ever thought of it. He wrote me what people call "a beautiful letter;" he was kind; considerate, decently commiserating; then, after a few weeks, he slipped into his old way of coming in every afternoon, and our interminable talks began again just where they had left off. I heard later that people thought I had shown "such good taste" in not marrying him.

So we jogged on for five years longer. Perhaps they were the best years, for I had given up hoping. Then he died.

After his death--this is curious--there came to me a kind of mirage of love. All the books and articles written about him, all the reviews of the "Life," were full of discreet allusions to Silvia. I became again the Mrs. Anerton of the glorious days. Sentimental girls and dear lads like you turned pink when somebody whispered, "that was Silvia you were talking to." Idiots begged for my autograph--publishers urged me to write my reminiscences of him--critics consulted me about the reading of doubtful lines. And I knew that, to all these people, I was the woman Vincent Rendle had loved.

After a while that fire went out too and I was left alone with my past. Alone--quite alone; for he had never really been with me. The intellectual union counted for nothing now. It had been soul to soul, but never hand in hand, and there were no little things to remember him by.

Then there set in a kind of Arctic winter. I crawled into myself as into a snow-hut. I hated my solitude and yet dreaded any one who disturbed it. That phase, of course, passed like the others. I took up life again, and began to read the papers and consider the cut of my gowns. But there was one question that I could not be rid of, that haunted me night and day. Why had he never loved me? Why had I been so much to him, and no more? Was I so ugly, so essentially unlovable, that though a man might cherish me as his mind's comrade, he could not care for me as a woman? I can't tell you how that question tortured me. It became an obsession.

My poor friend, do you begin to see? I had to find out what some other man thought of me. Don't be too hard on me! Listen first--consider. When I first met Vincent Rendle I was a young woman, who had married early and led the quietest kind of life; I had had no "experiences." From the hour of our first meeting to the day of his death I never looked at any other man, and never noticed whether any other man looked at me. When he died, five years ago, I knew the extent of my powers no more than a baby. Was it too late to find out? Should I never know _why?_

Forgive me--forgive me. You are so young; it will be an episode, a mere "document," to you so soon! And, besides, it wasn't as deliberate, as cold-blooded as these disjointed lines have made it appear. I didn't plan it, like a woman in a book. Life is so much more complex than any rendering of it can be. I liked you from the first--I was drawn to you (you must have seen that)--I wanted you to like me; it was not a mere psychological experiment. And yet in a sense it was that, too--I must be honest. I had to have an answer to that question; it was a ghost that had to be laid.

At first I was afraid--oh, so much afraid--that you cared for me only because I was Silvia, that you loved me because you thought Rendle had loved me. I began to think there was no escaping my destiny.

How happy I was when I discovered that you were growing jealous of my past; that you actually hated Rendle! My heart beat like a girl's when you told me you meant to follow me to Venice.

After our parting at Villa d'Este my old doubts reasserted themselves. What did I know of your feeling for me, after all? Were you capable of analyzing it yourself? Was it not likely to be two-thirds vanity and curiosity, and one-third literary sentimentality? You might easily fancy that you cared for Mary Anerton when you were really in love with Silvia-- the heart is such a hypocrite! Or you might be more calculating than I had supposed. Perhaps it was you who had been flattering _my_ vanity in the hope (the pardonable hope!) of turning me, after a decent interval, into a pretty little essay with a margin.

When you arrived in Venice and we met again--do you remember the music on the lagoon, that evening, from my balcony?--I was so afraid you would begin to talk about the book--the book, you remember, was your ostensible reason for coming. You never spoke of it, and I soon saw your one fear was _I_ might do so--might remind you of your object in being with me. Then I knew you cared for me! yes, at that moment really cared! We never mentioned the book once, did we, during that month in Venice?

I have read my letter over; and now I wish that I had said this to you instead of writing it. I could have felt my way then, watching your face and seeing if you understood. But, no, I could not go back to Venice; and I could not tell you (though I tried) while we were there together. I couldn't spoil that month--my one month. It was so good, for once in my life, to get away from literature....

You will be angry with me at first--but, alas! not for long. What I have done would have been cruel if I had been a younger woman; as it is, the experiment will hurt no one but myself. And it will hurt me horribly (as much as, in your first anger, you may perhaps wish), because it has shown me, for the first time, all that I have missed....

The Letters

I

For many years he had lived withdrawn from the world in which he had once played so active and even turbulent a part. The study of Tuscan art was his only pursuit, and it was to help him in the classification of his notes and documents that I was first called to his villa. Colonel Alingdon had then the look of a very old man, though his age can hardly have exceeded seventy. He was small and bent, with a finely wrinkled face which still wore the tan of youthful exposure. But for this dusky redness it would have been hard to reconstruct from the shrunken recluse, with his low fastidious voice and carefully tended hands, an image of that young knight of adventure whose sword had been at the service of every uprising which stirred the uneasy soil of Italy in the first half of the nineteenth century.

Though I was more of a proficient in Colonel Alingdon's later than his earlier pursuits, the thought of his soldiering days was always coming between me and the pacific work of his old age. As we sat collating papers and comparing photographs, I had the feeling that this dry and quiet old man had seen even stranger things than people said: that he knew more of the inner history of Europe than half the diplomatists of his day.

I was not alone in this conviction; and the friend who had engaged me for Colonel Alingdon had appended to his instructions the injunction to "get him to talk." But this was what no one could do. Colonel Alingdon was ready to discuss by the hour the date of a Giottesque triptych, or the attribution of a disputed master; but on the history of his early life he was habitually silent.

It was perhaps because I recognized this silence and respected it that it afterward came to be broken for me. Or it was perhaps merely because, as the failure of Colonel Alingdon's sight cut him off from his work, he felt the natural inclination of age to revert from the empty present to the crowded past. For one cause or another he _did_ talk to me in the last year of his life; and I felt myself mingled, to an extent inconceivable to the mere reader of history, with the passionate scenes of the Italian struggle for liberty. Colonel Alingdon had been mixed with it in all its phases: he had known the last Carbonari and the Young Italy of Mazzini; he had been in Perugia when the mercenaries of a liberal Pope slaughtered women and children in the streets; he had been in Sicily with the Thousand, and in Milan during the _Cinque Giornate_.

"They say the Italians didn't know how to fight," he said one day, musingly--"that the French had to come down and do their work for them. People forget how long it was since they had had any fighting to do. But they hadn't forgotten how to suffer and hold their tongues; how to die and take their secrets with them. The Italian war of independence was really carried on underground: it was one of those awful silent struggles which are so much more terrible than the roar of a battle. It's a deuced sight easier to charge with your regiment than to lie rotting in an Austrian prison and know that if you give up the name of a friend or two you can go back scot-free to your wife and children. And thousands and thousands of Italians had the choice given them--and hardly one went back."

He sat silent, his meditative fingertips laid together, his eyes fixed on the past which was the now only thing clearly visible to them.

"And the women?" I said. "Were they as brave as the men?"

I had not spoken quite at random. I had always heard that there had been as much of love as of war in Colonel Alingdon's early career, and I hoped that my question might give a personal turn to his reminiscences.

"The women?" he repeated. "They were braver--for they had more to bear and less to do. Italy could never have been saved without them."

His eye had kindled and I detected in it the reflection of some vivid memory. It was then that I asked him what was the bravest thing he had ever known of a woman's doing.

The question was such a vague one that I hardly knew why I had put it, but to my surprise he answered almost at once, as though I had touched on a subject of frequent meditation.

"The bravest thing I ever saw done by a woman," he said, "was brought about by an act of my own--and one of which I am not particularly proud. For that reason I have never spoken of it before--there was a time when I didn't even care to think of it--but all that is past now. She died years ago, and so did the Jack Alingdon she knew, and in telling you the story I am no more than the mouthpiece of an old tradition which some ancestor might have handed down to me."

He leaned back, his clear blind gaze fixed smilingly on me, and I had the feeling that, in groping through the labyrinth of his young adventures, I had come unawares upon their central point.

II

When I was in Milan in 'forty-seven an unlucky thing happened to me.

I had been sent there to look over the ground by some of my Italian friends in England. As an English officer I had no difficulty in getting into Milanese society, for England had for years been the refuge of the Italian fugitives, and I was known to be working in their interests. It was just the kind of job I liked, and I never enjoyed life more than I did in those days. There was a great deal going on--good music, balls and theatres. Milan kept up her gayety to the last. The English were shocked by the _insouciance_ of a race who could dance under the very nose of the usurper; but those who understood the situation knew that Milan was playing Brutus, and playing it uncommonly well.

I was in the thick of it all--it was just the atmosphere to suit a young fellow of nine-and-twenty, with a healthy passion for waltzing and fighting. But, as I said, an unlucky thing happened to me. I was fool enough to fall in love with

Donna Candida Falco. You have heard of her, of course: you know the share she had in the great work. In a different way she was what the terrible Princess Belgioioso had been to an earlier generation. But Donna Candida was not terrible. She was quiet, discreet and charming. When I knew her she was a widow of thirty, her husband, Andrea Falco, having died ten years previously, soon after their marriage. The marriage had been notoriously unhappy, and his death was a release to Donna Candida. Her family were of Modena, but they had come to live in Milan soon after the execution of Ciro Menotti and his companions. You remember the details of that business? The Duke of Modena, one of the most adroit villains in Europe, had been bitten with the hope of uniting the Italian states under his rule. It was a vision of Italian liberation--of a sort. A few madmen were dazzled by it, and Ciro Menotti was one of them. You know the end. The Duke of Modena, who had counted on Louis Philippe's backing, found that that astute sovereign had betrayed him to Austria. Instantly, he saw that his first business was to get rid of the conspirators he had created. There was nothing easier than for a Hapsburg Este to turn on a friend. Ciro Menotti had staked his life for the Duke--and the Duke took it. You may remember that, on the night when seven hundred men and a cannon attacked Menotti's house, the Duke was seen looking on at the slaughter from an arcade across the square.

Well, among the lesser fry taken that night was a lad of eighteen, Emilio Verna, who was the only brother of Donna Candida. The Verna family was one of the most respected in Modena. It consisted, at that time, of the mother, Countess Verna, of young Emilio and his sister. Count Verna had been in Spielberg in the twenties. He had never recovered from his sufferings there, and died in exile, without seeing his wife and children again. Countess Verna had been an ardent patriot in her youth, but the failure of the first attempts against Austria had discouraged her. She thought that in losing her husband she had sacrificed enough for her country, and her one idea was to keep Emilio on good terms with the government. But the Verna blood was not tractable, and his father's death was not likely to make Emilio a good subject of the Estes. Not that he had as yet taken any active share in the work of the conspirators: he simply hadn't had time. At his trial there was nothing to show that he had been in Menotti's confidence; but he had been seen once or twice coming out of what the ducal police called "suspicious" houses, and in his desk were found some verses to Italy. That was enough to hang a man in Modena, and Emilio Verna was hanged.

The Countess never recovered from the blow. The circumstances of her son's death were too abominable, to unendurable. If he had risked his life in the conspiracy, she might have been reconciled to his losing it. But he was a mere child, who had sat at home, chafing but powerless, while his seniors plotted and fought. He had been sacrificed to the Duke's insane fear, to his savage greed for victims, and the Countess Verna was not to be consoled.

As soon as possible, the mother and daughter left Modena for Milan. There they lived in seclusion till Candida's marriage. During her girlhood she had had to accept her mother's view of life: to shut herself up in the tomb in which the poor woman brooded over her martyrs. But that was not the girl's way of honoring the dead. At the moment when the first shot was fired on Menotti's house she had been reading Petrarch's Ode to the Lords of Italy, and the lines _l'antico valor Ne Vitalici cor non e ancor morto_ had lodged like a bullet in her brain. From the day of her marriage she began to take a share in the silent work which was going on throughout Italy. Milan was at that time the centre of the movement, and Candida Falco threw herself into it with all the passion which her unhappy marriage left unsatisfied. At first she had to act with great reserve, for her husband was a prudent man, who did not care to have his habits disturbed by political complications; but after his death there was nothing to restrain her, except the exquisite tact which enabled her to work night and day in the Italian cause without giving the Austrian authorities a pretext for interference.

When I first knew Donna Candida, her mother was still living: a tragic woman, prematurely bowed, like an image of death in the background of the daughter's brilliant life. The Countess, since her son's death, had become a patriot again, though in a narrower sense than Candida. The mother's first thought was that her dead must be avenged, the daughter's that Italy must be saved; but from different motives they worked for the same end. Candida felt for the Countess that protecting tenderness with which Italian children so often regard their parents, a feeling heightened by the reverence which the mother's sufferings inspired. Countess Verna, as the wife and mother of martyrs, had done what Candida longed to do: she had given her utmost to Italy. There must have been moments when the self-absorption of her grief chilled her daughter's ardent spirit; but Candida revered in her mother the image of their afflicted country.

"It was too terrible," she said, speaking of what the Countess had suffered after Emilio's death. "All the circumstances were too unmerciful. It seemed as if God had turned His face from my mother; as if she had been singled out to suffer more than any of the others. All the other families received some message or token of farewell from the prisoners. One of them bribed the gaoler to carry a letter--another sent a lock of hair by the chaplain. But Emilio made no sign, sent no word. My mother felt as though he had turned his back on us. She used to sit for hours, saying again and again, 'Why was he the only one to forget his mother?' I tried to comfort her, but it was useless: she had suffered too much. Now I never reason with her; I listen, and let her ease her poor heart. Do you know, she still asks me sometimes if I think he may have left a letter--if there is no way of finding out if he left one? She forgets that I have tried again and again: that I have sent bribes and messages to the gaoler, the chaplain, to every one who came near him. The answer is always the same--no one has ever heard of a letter. I suppose the poor boy was stunned, and did not think of writing. Who knows what was passing through his poor bewildered brain? But it would have been a great help to my mother to have a word from him. If I had known how to imitate his writing I should have forged a letter."

I knew enough of the Italians to understand how her boy's silence must have aggravated the Countess's grief. Precious as a message from a dying son would be to any mother, such signs of tenderness have to the Italians a peculiar significance. The Latin race is rhetorical: it possesses the gift of death-bed eloquence, the knack of saying the effective thing on momentous occasions. The letters which the Italian patriots sent home from their prisons or from the scaffold are not the halting farewells that anguish would have wrung from a less expressive race: they are veritable "compositions," saved from affectation only by the fact that fluency and sonority are a part of the Latin inheritance. Such letters, passed from hand to hand among the bereaved families, were not only a comfort to the survivors but an incentive to fresh sacrifices. They were the "seed of the martyrs" with which Italy was being sown; and I knew what it meant to the Countess Verna to have no such treasure in her bosom, to sit silent while other mothers quoted their sons' last words.

I said just now that it was an unlucky day for me when I fell in love with Donna Candida; and no doubt you have guessed the reason. She was in love with some one else. It was the old situation of Heine's song. That other loved another--loved Italy, and with an undivided passion. His name was Fernando Briga, and at that time he was one of the foremost liberals in Italy. He came of a middle-class Modenese family. His father was a doctor, a prudent man, engrossed in his profession and unwilling to compromise it by meddling in politics. His irreproachable attitude won the confidence of the government, and the Duke conferred on him the sinister office of physician to the prisons of Modena. It was this Briga who attended Emilio Falco, and several of the other prisoners who were executed at the same time.

Under shelter of his father's loyalty young Fernando conspired in safety. He was studying medicine, and every one supposed him to be absorbed in his work; but as a matter of fact he was fast ripening into one of Mazzini's ablest lieutenants. His career belongs to history, so I need not enlarge on it here. In 1847 he was in Milan, and had become one of the leading figures in the liberal group which was working for a coalition with Piedmont. Like all the ablest men of his day, he had cast off Mazziniism and pinned his faith to the house of Savoy. The Austrian government had an eye on him, but he had inherited his father's prudence, though he used it for nobler ends, and his discretion enabled him to do far more for the cause than a dozen enthusiasts could have accomplished. No one understood this better than Donna Candida. She had a share of his caution, and he trusted her with secrets which he would not have confided to many men. Her drawing-room was the centre of the Piedmontese party, yet so clever was she in averting suspicion that more than one hunted conspirator hid in her house, and was helped across the Alps by her agents.

Briga relied on her as he did on no one else; but he did not love her, and she knew it. Still, she was young, she was handsome, and he loved no one else: how could she give up hoping? From her intimate friends she made no secret of her feelings: Italian women are not reticent in such matters, and Donna Candida was proud of loving a hero. You will see at once that I had no chance; but if she could not give up hope, neither could I. Perhaps in her desire to secure my services for the cause she may have shown herself overkind; or perhaps I was still young enough to set down to my own charms a success due to quite different causes. At any rate, I persuaded myself that if I could manage to do something conspicuous for Italy I might yet make her care for me. With such an incentive you will not wonder that I worked hard; but though Donna Candida was full of gratitude she continued to adore my rival.

One day we had a hot scene. I began, I believe, by reproaching her with having led me on; and when she defended herself, I retaliated by taunting her with Briga's indifference. She grew pale at that, and said it was enough to love a hero, even without hope of return; and as she said it she herself looked so heroic, so radiant, so unattainably the woman I wanted, that a sneer may have escaped me:--was she so sure then that Briga was a hero? I remember her proud silence and our wretched parting. I went away feeling that at last I had really lost her; and the thought made me savage and vindictive.

Soon after, as it happened, came the _Five Days_, and Milan was free. I caught a distant glimpse of Donna Candida in the hospital to which I was carried after the fight; but my wound was a slight one and in twenty-four hours I was about again on crutches. I hoped she might send for me, but she did not, and I was too sulky to make the first advance. A day or two later I heard there had been a commotion in Modena, and not being in fighting trim I got leave to go over there with one or two men whom the Modenese liberals had called in to help them. When we arrived the precious Duke had been swept out and a provisional government set up. One of my companions, who was a Modenese, was made a member, and knowing that I wanted something to do, he commissioned me to look up some papers in the ducal archives. It was fascinating work, for in the pursuit of my documents I uncovered the hidden springs of his late Highness's paternal administration. The principal papers relative to the civil and criminal administration of Modena have since been published, and the world knows how that estimable sovereign cared for the material and spiritual welfare of his subjects.

Well--in the course of my search, I came across a file of old papers marked: "Taken from political prisoners. A.D. 1831." It was the year of Menotti's conspiracy, and everything connected with that date was thrilling. I loosened the band and ran over the letters. Suddenly I came across one which was docketed: “Given by Doctor Briga’s son to the warder of His Highness’s prisons.” _Doctor Briga’s son?_ That could be no other than Fernando: I knew he was an only child. But how came such a paper into his hands, and how had it passed from them into those of the Duke’s warder? My own hands shook as I opened the letter--I felt the man suddenly in my power.

Then I began to read. “My adored mother, even in this lowest circle of hell all hearts are not closed to pity, and I have been given the hope that these last words of farewell may reach you....” My eyes ran on over pages of plaintive rhetoric. “Embrace for me my adored Candida...let her never forget the cause for which her father and brother perished... let her keep alive in her breast the thought of Spielberg and Reggio. Do not grieve that I die so young... though not with those heroes in deed I was with them in spirit, and am worthy to be enrolled in the sacred phalanx...” and so on. Before I reached the signature I knew the letter was from Emilio Verna.

I put it in my pocket, finished my work and started immediately for Milan. I didn’t quite know what I meant to do--my head was in a whirl. I saw at once what must have happened. Fernando Briga, then a lad of fifteen or sixteen, had attended his father in prison during Emilio Verna’s last hours, and the latter, perhaps aware of the lad’s liberal sympathies, had found an opportunity of giving him the letter. But why had Briga given it up to the warder? That was the puzzling question. The docket said: “_ Given by_ Doctor Briga’s son”--but it might mean “taken from.” Fernando might have been seen to receive the letter and might have been searched on leaving the prison. But that would not account for his silence afterward. How was it that, if he knew of the letter, he had never told Emilio's family of it? There was only one explanation. If the letter had been taken from him by force he would have had no reason for concealing its existence; and his silence was clear proof that he had given it up voluntarily, no doubt in the hope of standing well with the authorities. But then he was a traitor and a coward; the patriot of 'forty-eight had begun life as an informer! But does innate character ever change so radically that the lad who has committed a base act at fifteen may grow up into an honorable man? A good man may be corrupted by life, but can the years turn a born sneak into a hero?

You may fancy how I answered my own questions....If Briga had been false and cowardly then, was he not sure to be false and cowardly still? In those days there were traitors under every coat, and more than one brave fellow had been sold to the police by his best friend....You will say that Briga's record was unblemished, that he had exposed himself to danger too frequently, had stood by his friends too steadfastly, to permit of a rational doubt of his good faith. So reason might have told me in a calmer moment, but she was not allowed to make herself heard just then. I was young, I was angry, I chose to think I had been unfairly treated, and perhaps at my rival's instigation. It was not unlikely that Briga knew of my love for Donna Candida, and had encouraged her to use it in the good cause. Was she not always at his bidding? My blood boiled at the thought, and reaching Milan in a rage I went straight to Donna Candida.

I had measured the exact force of the blow I was going to deal. The triumph of the liberals in Modena had revived public interest in the unsuccessful struggle of their predecessors, the men who, sixteen years earlier, had paid for the same attempt with their lives. The victors of 'forty-eight wished to honor the vanquished of 'thirty-two. All the families exiled by the ducal government were hastening back to recover possession of their confiscated property and of the graves of their dead. Already it had been decided to raise a monument to Menotti and his companions. There were to be speeches, garlands, a public holiday: the thrill of the commemoration would run through Europe. You see what it would have meant to the poor Countess to appear on the scene with her boy's letter in her hand; and you see also what the memorandum on the back of the letter would have meant to Donna Candida. Poor Emilio's farewell would be published in all the journals of Europe: the finding of the letter would be on every one's lips. And how conceal those fatal words on the back? At the moment, it seemed to me that fortune could not have given me a handsomer chance of destroying my rival than in letting me find the letter which he stood convicted of having suppressed.

My sentiment was perhaps not a strictly honorable one; yet what could I do but give the letter to Donna Candida? To keep it back was out of the question; and with the best will in the world I could not have erased Briga's name from the back. The mistake I made was in thinking it lucky that the paper had fallen into my hands.

Donna Candida was alone when I entered. We had parted in anger, but she held out her hand with a smile of pardon, and asked what news I brought from Modena. The smile exasperated me: I felt as though she were trying to get me into her power again.

"I bring you a letter from your brother," I said, and handed it to her. I had purposely turned the superscription downward, so that she should not see it.

She uttered an incredulous cry and tore the letter open. A light struck up from it into her face as she read--a radiance that smote me to the soul. For a moment I longed to snatch the paper from her and efface the name on the back. It hurt me to think how short-lived her happiness must be.

Then she did a fatal thing. She came up to me, caught my two hands and kissed them. "Oh, thank you--bless you a thousand times! He died thinking of us--he died loving Italy!"

I put her from me gently: it was not the kiss I wanted, and the touch of her lips hardened me.

She shone on me through her happy tears. "What happiness--what consolation you have brought my poor mother! This will take the bitterness from her grief. And that it should come to her now! Do you know, she had a presentiment of it? When we heard of the Duke's flight her first word was: 'Now we may find Emilio's letter.' At heart she was always sure that he had written--I suppose some blessed instinct told her so." She dropped her face on her hands, and I saw her tears fall on the wretched letter.

In a moment she looked up again, with eyes that blessed and trusted me. "Tell me where you found it," she said.

I told her.

"Oh, the savages! They took it from him--"

My opportunity had come. "No," I said, "it appears they did _not_ take it from him."

"Then how--"

I waited a moment. "The letter," I said, looking full at her, "was given up to the warder of the prison by the son of Doctor Briga."

She stared, repeating the words slowly. "The son of Doctor Briga? But that is--Fernando," she said.

"I have always understood," I replied, "that your friend was an only son."

I had expected an outcry of horror; if she had uttered it I could have forgiven her anything. But I heard, instead, an incredulous exclamation: my statement was really too preposterous! I saw that her mind had flashed back to our last talk, and that she charged me with something too nearly true to be endurable.

"My brother's letter? Given to the prison warder by Fernando Briga? My dear Captain Alingdon--on what authority do you expect me to believe such a tale?"

Her incredulity had in it an evident implication of bad faith, and I was stung to a quick reply.

"If you will turn over the letter you will see."

She continued to gaze at me a moment: then she obeyed. I don't think I ever admired her more than I did then. As she read the name a tremor crossed her face; and that was all. Her mind must have reached out instantly to the farthest consequences of the discovery, but the long habit of self-command enabled her to steady her muscles at once. If I had not been on the alert I should have seen no hint of emotion.

For a while she looked fixedly at the back of the letter; then she raised her eyes to mine.

"Can you tell me who wrote this?" she asked.

Her composure irritated me. She had rallied all her forces to Briga's defence, and I felt as though my triumph were slipping from me.

"Probably one of the clerks of the archives," I answered. "It is written in the same hand as all the other memoranda relating to the political prisoners of that year."

"But it is a lie!" she exclaimed. "He was never admitted to the prisons."

"Are you sure?"

"How should he have been?"

"He might have gone as his father's assistant."

"But if he had seen my poor brother he would have told me long ago."

"Not if he had really given up this letter," I retorted.

I supposed her quick intelligence had seized this from the first; but I saw now that it came to her as a shock. She stood motionless, clenching the letter in her hands, and I could guess the rapid travel of her thoughts.

Suddenly she came up to me. "Colonel Alingdon," she said, "you have been a good friend of mine, though I think you have not liked me lately. But whether you like me or not, I know you will not deceive me. On your honor, do you think this memorandum may have been written later than the letter?"

I hesitated. If she had cried out once against Briga I should have wished myself out of the business; but she was too sure of him.

"On my honor," I said, "I think it hardly possible. The ink has faded to the same degree."

She made a rapid comparison and folded the letter with a gesture of assent.

"It may have been written by an enemy," I went on, wishing to clear myself of any appearance of malice.

She shook her head. "He was barely fifteen--and his father was on the side of the government. Besides, this would have served him with the government, and the liberals would never have known of it."

This was unanswerable--and still not a word of revolt against the man whose condemnation she was pronouncing!

"Then--" I said with a vague gesture.

She caught me up. "Then--?"

"You have answered my objections," I returned.

"Your objections?"

"To thinking that Signor Briga could have begun his career as a patriot by betraying a friend."

I had brought her to the test at last, but my eyes shrank from her face as I spoke. There was a dead silence, which I broke by adding lamely: "But no doubt Signor Briga could explain."

She lifted her head, and I saw that my triumph was to be short. She stood erect, a few paces from me, resting her hand on a table, but not for support.

"Of course he can explain," she said; "do you suppose I ever doubted it? But--" she paused a moment, fronting me nobly--"he need not, for I understand it all now."

"Ah," I murmured with a last flicker of irony.

"I understand," she repeated. It was she, now, who sought my eyes and held them. "It is quite simple--he could not have done otherwise."

This was a little too oracular to be received with equanimity. I suppose I smiled.

"He could not have done otherwise," she repeated with tranquil emphasis. "He merely did what is every Italian's duty--he put Italy before himself and his friends." She waited a moment, and then went on with growing passion: "Surely you must see what I mean? He was evidently in the prison with his father at the time of my poor brother's death. Emilio perhaps guessed that he was a friend--or perhaps appealed to him because he was young and looked kind. But don't you see how dangerous it would have been for Briga to bring this letter to us, or even to hide it in his father's house? It is true that he was not yet suspected of liberalism, but he was already connected with Young Italy, and it is just because he managed to keep himself so free of suspicion that he was able to do such good work for the cause." She paused, and then went on with a firmer voice. "You don't know the danger we all lived in. The government spies were everywhere. The laws were set aside as the Duke pleased--was not Emilio hanged for having an ode to Italy in his desk? After Menotti's conspiracy the Duke grew mad with fear--he was haunted by the dread of assassination. The police, to prove their zeal, had to trump up false charges and arrest innocent persons--you remember the case of poor Ricci? Incriminating papers were smuggled into people's houses--they were condemned to death on the paid evidence of brigands and galley-slaves. The families of the revolutionists were under the closest observation and were shunned by all who wished to stand well with the government. If Briga had been seen going into our house he would at once have been suspected. If he had hidden Emilio's letter at home, its discovery might have ruined his family as well as himself. It was his duty to consider all these things. In those days no man could serve two masters, and he had to choose between endangering the cause and failing to serve a friend. He chose the latter--and he was right."

I stood listening, fascinated by the rapidity and skill with which she had built up the hypothesis of Briga's defence. But before she ended a strange thing happened--her argument had convinced me. It seemed to me quite likely that Briga had in fact been actuated by the motives she suggested.

I suppose she read the admission in my face, for hers lit up victoriously.

"You see?" she exclaimed. "Ah, it takes one brave man to understand another."

Perhaps I winced a little at being thus coupled with her hero; at any rate, some last impulse of resistance made me say: "I should be quite convinced, if Briga had only spoken of the letter afterward. If brave people understand each other, I cannot see why he should have been afraid of telling you the truth."

She colored deeply, and perhaps not quite resentfully.

"You are right," she said; "he need not have been afraid. But he does not know me as I know him. I was useful to Italy, and he may have feared to risk my friendship."

"You are the most generous woman I ever knew!" I exclaimed.

She looked at me intently. "You also are generous," she said.

I stiffened instantly, suspecting a purpose behind her praise. "I have given you small proof of it!" I said.

She seemed surprised. "In bringing me this letter? What else could you do?" She sighed deeply. "You can give me proof enough now."

She had dropped into a chair, and I saw that we had reached the most difficult point in our interview.

"Captain Alingdon," she said, "does any one else know of this letter?"

"No. I was alone in the archives when I found it."

"And you spoke of it to no one?"

"To no one."

"Then no one must know."

I bowed. "It is for you to decide."

She paused. "Not even my mother," she continued, with a painful blush.

I looked at her in amazement. "Not even--?"

She shook her head sadly. "You think me a cruel daughter? Well--_he_ was a cruel friend. What he did was done for Italy: shall I allow myself to be surpassed?"

I felt a pang of commiseration for the mother. "But you will at least tell the Countess--"

Her eyes filled with tears. "My poor mother--don't make it more difficult for me!"

"But I don't understand--"

"Don't you see that she might find it impossible to forgive him? She has suffered so much! And I can't risk that--for in her anger she might speak. And even if she forgave him, she might be tempted to show the letter. Don't you see that, even now, a word of this might ruin him? I will trust his fate to no one. If Italy needed him then she needs him far more to-day."

She stood before me magnificently, in the splendor of her great refusal; then she turned to the writing-table at which she had been seated when I came in. Her sealing-taper was still alight, and she held her brother's letter to the flame.

I watched her in silence while it burned; but one more question rose to my lips.

"You will tell _him_, then, what you have done for him?" I cried.

And at that the heroine turned woman, melted and pressed unhappy hands in mine.

"Don't you see that I can never tell him what I do for him? That is my gift to Italy," she said.

The Dilettante.

IT was on an impulse hardly needing the arguments he found himself advancing in its favor, that Thursdale, on his way to the club, turned as usual into Mrs. Vervain's street.

The "as usual" was his own qualification of the act; a convenient way of bridging the interval--in days and other sequences--that lay between this visit and the last. It was characteristic of him that he instinctively excluded his call two days earlier, with Ruth Gaynor, from the list of his visits to Mrs. Vervain: the special conditions attending it had made it no more like a visit to Mrs. Vervain than an engraved dinner invitation is like a personal letter. Yet it was to talk over his call with Miss Gaynor that he was now returning to the scene of that episode; and it was because Mrs. Vervain could be trusted to handle the talking over as skilfully as the interview itself that, at her corner, he had felt the dilettante's irresistible craving to take a last look at a work of art that was passing out of his possession.

On the whole, he knew no one better fitted to deal with the unexpected than Mrs. Vervain. She excelled in the rare art of taking things for granted, and Thursdale felt a pardonable pride in the thought that she owed her excellence to his training. Early in his career Thursdale had made the mistake, at the outset of his acquaintance with a lady, of telling her that he loved her and exacting the same avowal in return. The latter part of that episode had been like the long walk back from a picnic, when one has to carry all the crockery one has finished using: it was the last time Thursdale ever allowed himself to be encumbered with the debris of a feast. He thus incidentally learned that the privilege of loving her is one of the least favors that a charming woman can accord; and in seeking to avoid the pitfalls of sentiment he had developed a science of evasion in which the woman of the moment became a mere implement of the game. He owed a great deal of delicate enjoyment to the cultivation of this art. The perils from which it had been his refuge became naively harmless: was it possible that he who now took his easy way along the levels had once preferred to gasp on the raw heights of emotion? Youth is a high-colored season; but he had the satisfaction of feeling that he had entered earlier than most into that chiar'oscuro of sensation where every half-tone has its value.

As a promoter of this pleasure no one he had known was comparable to Mrs. Vervain. He had taught a good many women not to betray their feelings, but he had never before had such fine material to work in. She had been surprisingly crude when he first knew her; capable of making the most awkward inferences, of plunging through thin ice, of recklessly undressing her emotions; but she had acquired, under the discipline of his reticences and evasions, a skill almost equal to his own, and perhaps more remarkable in that it involved keeping time with any tune he played and reading at sight some uncommonly difficult passages.

It had taken Thursdale seven years to form this fine talent; but the result justified the effort. At the crucial moment she had been perfect: her way of greeting Miss Gaynor had made him regret that he had announced his engagement by letter. it was an evasion that confessed a difficulty; a deviation implying an obstacle, where, by common consent, it was agreed to see none; it betrayed, in short, a lack of confidence in the completeness of his method. It had been his pride never to put himself in a position which had to be quitted, as it were, by the back door; but here, as he perceived, the main portals would have opened for him of their own accord. All this, and much more, he read in the finished naturalness with which Mrs. Vervain had met Miss Gaynor. He had never seen a better piece of work: there was no over-eagerness, no suspicious warmth, above all (and this gave her art the grace of a natural quality) there were none of those damnable implications whereby a woman, in welcoming her friend's betrothed, may keep him on pins and needles while she laps the lady in complacency. So masterly a performance, indeed, hardly needed the offset of Miss Gaynor's door-step words--"To be so kind to me, how she must have liked you!"--though he caught himself wishing it lay within the bounds of fitness to transmit them, as a final tribute, to the one woman he knew who was unfailingly certain to enjoy a good thing. It was perhaps the one drawback to his new situation that it might develop good things which it would be impossible to hand on to Margaret Vervain.

The fact that he had made the mistake of underrating his friend's powers, the consciousness that his writing must have betrayed his distrust of her efficiency, seemed an added reason for turning down her street instead of going on to the club. He would show her that he knew how to value her; he would ask her to achieve with him a feat infinitely rarer and more delicate than the one he had appeared to avoid. Incidentally, he would also dispose of the interval of time before dinner: ever since he had seen Miss Gaynor off, an hour earlier, on her return journey to Buffalo, he had been wondering how he should put in the rest of the afternoon. It was absurd, how he missed the girl....Yes, that was it; the desire to talk about her was, after all, at the bottom of his impulse to call on Mrs. Vervain! It was absurd, if you like--but it was delightfully rejuvenating. He could recall the time when he had been afraid of being obvious: now he felt that this return to the primitive emotions might be as restorative as a holiday in the Canadian woods. And it was precisely by the girl's candor, her directness, her lack of complications, that he was taken. The sense that she might say something rash at any moment was positively exhilarating: if she had thrown her arms about him at the station he would not have given a thought to his crumpled dignity. It surprised Thursdale to find what freshness of heart he brought to the adventure; and though his sense of irony prevented his ascribing his intactness to any conscious purpose, he could but rejoice in the fact that his sentimental economies had left him such a large surplus to draw upon.

Mrs. Vervain was at home--as usual. When one visits the cemetery one expects to find the angel on the tombstone, and it struck Thursdale as another proof of his friend's good taste that she had been in no undue haste to change her habits. The whole house appeared to count on his coming; the footman took his hat and overcoat as naturally as though there had been no lapse in his visits; and the drawing-room at once enveloped him in that atmosphere of tacit intelligence which Mrs. Vervain imparted to her very furniture.

It was a surprise that, in this general harmony of circumstances, Mrs. Vervain should herself sound the first false note.

"You?" she exclaimed; and the book she held slipped from her hand.

It was crude, certainly; unless it were a touch of the finest art. The difficulty of classifying it disturbed Thursdale's balance.

"Why not?" he said, restoring the book. "Isn't it my hour?" And as she made no answer, he added gently, "Unless it's some one else's?"

She laid the book aside and sank back into her chair. "Mine, merely," she said.

"I hope that doesn't mean that you're unwilling to share it?"

"With you? By no means. You're welcome to my last crust."

He looked at her reproachfully. "Do you call this the last?"

She smiled as he dropped into the seat across the hearth. "It's a way of giving it more flavor!"

He returned the smile. "A visit to you doesn't need such condiments."

She took this with just the right measure of retrospective amusement.

"Ah, but I want to put into this one a very special taste," she confessed.

Her smile was so confident, so reassuring, that it lulled him into the imprudence of saying, "Why should you want it to be different from what was always so perfectly right?"

She hesitated. "Doesn't the fact that it's the last constitute a difference?"

"The last--my last visit to you?"

"Oh, metaphorically, I mean--there's a break in the continuity."

Decidedly, she was pressing too hard: unlearning his arts already!

"I don't recognize it," he said. "Unless you make me--" he added, with a note that slightly stirred her attitude of languid attention.

She turned to him with grave eyes. "You recognize no difference whatever?"

"None--except an added link in the chain."

"An added link?"

"In having one more thing to like you for--your letting Miss Gaynor see why I had already so many." He flattered himself that this turn had taken the least hint of fatuity from the phrase.

Mrs. Vervain sank into her former easy pose. "Was it that you came for?" she asked, almost gaily.

"If it is necessary to have a reason--that was one."

"To talk to me about Miss Gaynor?"

"To tell you how she talks about you."

"That will be very interesting--especially if you have seen her since her second visit to me."

"Her second visit?" Thursdale pushed his chair back with a start and moved to another. "She came to see you again?"

"This morning, yes--by appointment."

He continued to look at her blankly. "You sent for her?"

"I didn't have to--she wrote and asked me last night. But no doubt you have seen her since."

Thursdale sat silent. He was trying to separate his words from his thoughts, but they still clung together inextricably. "I saw her off just now at the station."

"And she didn't tell you that she had been here again?"

"There was hardly time, I suppose--there were people about--" he floundered.

"Ah, she'll write, then."

He regained his composure. "Of course she'll write: very often, I hope. You know I'm absurdly in love," he cried audaciously.

She tilted her head back, looking up at him as he leaned against the chimney-piece. He had leaned there so often that the attitude touched a pulse which set up a throbbing in her throat. "Oh, my poor Thursdale!" she murmured.

"I suppose it's rather ridiculous," he owned; and as she remained silent, he added, with a sudden break--"Or have you another reason for pitying me?"

Her answer was another question. "Have you been back to your rooms since you left her?"

"Since I left her at the station? I came straight here."

"Ah, yes--you _could:_ there was no reason--" Her words passed into a silent musing.

Thursdale moved nervously nearer. "You said you had something to tell me?"

"Perhaps I had better let her do so. There may be a letter at your rooms."

"A letter? What do you mean? A letter from _her?_ What has happened?"

His paleness shook her, and she raised a hand of reassurance. "Nothing has happened--perhaps that is just the worst of it. You always _hated_, you know," she added incoherently, "to have things happen: you never would let them."

"And now--?"

"Well, that was what she came here for: I supposed you had guessed. To know if anything had happened."

"Had happened?" He gazed at her slowly. "Between you and me?" he said with a rush of light.

The words were so much cruder than any that had ever passed between them that the color rose to her face; but she held his startled gaze.

"You know girls are not quite as unsophisticated as they used to be. Are you surprised that such an idea should occur to her?"

His own color answered hers: it was the only reply that came to him.

Mrs. Vervain went on, smoothly: "I supposed it might have struck you that there were times when we presented that appearance."

He made an impatient gesture. "A man's past is his own!"

"Perhaps--it certainly never belongs to the woman who has shared it. But one learns such truths only by experience; and Miss Gaynor is naturally inexperienced."

"Of course--but--supposing her act a natural one--" he floundered lamentably among his innuendoes--"I still don't see--how there was anything--"

"Anything to take hold of? There wasn't--"

"Well, then--?" escaped him, in crude satisfaction; but as she did not complete the sentence he went on with a faltering laugh: "She can hardly object to the existence of a mere friendship between us!"

"But she does," said Mrs. Vervain.

Thursdale stood perplexed. He had seen, on the previous day, no trace of jealousy or resentment in his betrothed: he could still hear the candid ring of the girl's praise of Mrs. Vervain. If she were such an abyss of insincerity as to dissemble distrust under such frankness, she must at least be more subtle than to bring her doubts to her rival for solution. The situation seemed one through which one could no longer move in a penumbra, and he let in a burst of light with the direct query: "Won't you explain what you mean?"

Mrs. Vervain sat silent, not provokingly, as though to prolong his distress, but as if, in the attenuated phraseology he had taught her, it was difficult to find words robust enough to meet his challenge. It was the first time he had ever asked her to explain anything; and she had lived so long in dread of offering elucidations which were not wanted, that she seemed unable to produce one on the spot.

At last she said slowly: "She came to find out if you were really free."

Thursdale colored again. "Free?" he stammered, with a sense of physical disgust at contact with such crassness.

"Yes--if I had quite done with you." She smiled in recovered security. "It seems she likes clear outlines; she has a passion for definitions."

"Yes--well?" he said, wincing at the echo of his own subtlety.

"Well--and when I told her that you had never belonged to me, she wanted me to define _my_ status--to know exactly where I had stood all along."

Thursdale sat gazing at her intently; his hand was not yet on the clue. "And even when you had told her that--"

"Even when I had told her that I had _had_ no status--that I had never stood anywhere, in any sense she meant," said Mrs. Vervain, slowly--"even then she wasn't satisfied, it seems."

He uttered an uneasy exclamation. "She didn't believe you, you mean?"

"I mean that she _did_ believe me: too thoroughly."

"Well, then--in God's name, what did she want?"

"Something more--those were the words she used."

"Something more? Between--between you and me? Is it a conundrum?" He laughed awkwardly.

"Girls are not what they were in my day; they are no longer forbidden to contemplate the relation of the sexes."

"So it seems!" he commented. "But since, in this case, there wasn't any--" he broke off, catching the dawn of a revelation in her gaze.

"That's just it. The unpardonable offence has been--in our not offending."

He flung himself down despairingly. "I give it up!--What did you tell her?" he burst out with sudden crudeness.

"The exact truth. If I had only known," she broke off with a beseeching tenderness, "won't you believe that I would still have lied for you?"

"Lied for me? Why on earth should you have lied for either of us?"

"To save you--to hide you from her to the last! As I've hidden you from myself all these years!" She stood up with a sudden tragic import in her movement. "You believe me capable of that, don't you? If I had only guessed--but I have never known a girl like her; she had the truth out of me with a spring."

"The truth that you and I had never--"

"Had never--never in all these years! Oh, she knew why--she measured us both in a flash. She didn't suspect me of having haggled with you--her words pelted me like hail. 'He just took what he wanted--sifted and sorted you to suit his taste. Burnt out the gold and left a heap of cinders. And you let him--you let yourself be cut in bits'--she mixed her metaphors a little--'be cut in bits, and used or discarded, while all the while every drop of blood in you belonged to him! But he's Shylock--and you have bled to death of the pound of flesh he has cut out of you.' But she despises me the most, you know--far the most--" Mrs. Vervain ended.

The words fell strangely on the scented stillness of the room: they seemed out of harmony with its setting of afternoon intimacy, the kind of intimacy on which at any moment, a visitor might intrude without perceptibly lowering the atmosphere. It was as though a grand opera-singer had strained the acoustics of a private music-room.

Thursdale stood up, facing his hostess. Half the room was between them, but they seemed to stare close at each other now that the veils of reticence and ambiguity had fallen.

His first words were characteristic. "She _does_ despise me, then?" he exclaimed.

"She thinks the pound of flesh you took was a little too near the heart."

He was excessively pale. "Please tell me exactly what she said of me."

"She did not speak much of you: she is proud. But I gather that while she understands love or indifference, her eyes have never been opened to the many intermediate shades of feeling. At any rate, she expressed an unwillingness to be taken with reservations--she thinks you would have loved her better if you had loved some one else first. The point of view is original--she insists on a man with a past!"

"Oh, a past--if she's serious--I could rake up a past!" he said with a laugh.

"So I suggested: but she has her eyes on his particular portion of it. She insists on making it a test case. She wanted to know what you had done to me; and before I could guess her drift I blundered into telling her."

Thursdale drew a difficult breath. "I never supposed--your revenge is complete," he said slowly.

He heard a little gasp in her throat. "My revenge? When I sent for you to warn you--to save you from being surprised as _I_ was surprised?"

"You're very good--but it's rather late to talk of saving me." He held out his hand in the mechanical gesture of leave-taking.

"How you must care!--for I never saw you so dull," was

her answer. "Don't you see that it's not too late for me to help you?" And as he continued to stare, she brought out sublimely: "Take the rest--in imagination! Let it at least be of that much use to you. Tell her I lied to her--she's too ready to believe it! And so, after all, in a sense, I sha'n't have been wasted."

His stare hung on her, widening to a kind of wonder. She gave the look back brightly, unblushingly, as though the expedient were too simple to need oblique approaches. It was extraordinary how a few words had swept them from an atmosphere of the most complex dissimulations to this contact of naked souls.

It was not in Thursdale to expand with the pressure of fate; but something in him cracked with it, and the rift let in new light. He went up to his friend and took her hand.

"You would do it--you would do it!"

She looked at him, smiling, but her hand shook.

"Good-by," he said, kissing it.

"Good-by? You are going--?"

"To get my letter."

"Your letter? The letter won't matter, if you will only do what I ask."

He returned her gaze. "I might, I suppose, without being out of character. Only, don't you see that if your plan helped me it could only harm her?"

"Harm _her?_"

"To sacrifice you wouldn't make me different. I shall go on being what I have always been--sifting and sorting, as she calls it. Do you want my punishment to fall on _her?_"

She looked at him long and deeply. "Ah, if I had to choose between you--!"

"You would let her take her chance? But I can't, you see. I must take my punishment alone."

She drew her hand away, sighing. "Oh, there will be no punishment for either of you."

"For either of us? There will be the reading of her letter for me."

She shook her head with a slight laugh. "There will be no letter."

Thursdale faced about from the threshold with fresh life in his look. "No letter? You don't mean--"

"I mean that she's been with you since I saw her--she's seen you and heard your voice. If there _is_ a letter, she has recalled it--from the first station, by telegraph."

He turned back to the door, forcing an answer to her smile. "But in the mean while I shall have read it," he said.

The door closed on him, and she hid her eyes from the dreadful emptiness of the room.

The Pelican

SHE WAS VERY PRETTY WHEN I FIRST KNEW her, with the sweet straight nose and short upper lip of the cameo-brooch divinity, humanized by a dimple that flowered in her cheek whenever anything was said possessing the outward attributes of humor without its intrinsic quality. For the dear lady was providentially deficient in humor: the least hint of the real thing clouded her lovely eye like the hovering shadow of an algebraic problem.

I don't think nature had meant her to be "intellectual;" but what can a poor thing do, whose husband has died of drink when her baby is hardly six months old, and who finds her coral necklace and her grandfather's edition of the British Dramatists inadequate to the demands of the creditors?

Her mother, the celebrated Irene Astarte Pratt, had written a poem in blank verse on "The Fall of Man;" one of her aunts was dean of a girls' college; another had translated Euripides--with such a family, the poor child's fate was sealed in advance. The only way of paying her husband's debts and keeping the baby clothed was to be intellectual; and, after some hesitation as to the form her mental activity was to take, it was unanimously decided that she was to give lectures.

They began by being drawing-room lectures. The first time I saw her she was standing by the piano, against a flippant background of Dresden china and photographs, telling a roomful of women preoccupied with their spring bonnets all she thought she knew about Greek art. The ladies assembled to hear her had given me to understand that she was "doing it for the baby," and this fact, together with the shortness of her upper lip and the bewildering co-operation of her dimple, disposed me to listen leniently to her dissertation. Happily, at that time Greek art was still, if I may use the phrase, easily handled: it was as simple as walking down a museum- gallery lined with pleasant familiar Venuses and Apollos. All the later complications--the archaic and archaistic conundrums; the influences of Assyria and Asia Minor; the conflicting attributions and the wrangles of the erudite--still slumbered in the bosom of the future "scientific critic." Greek art in those days began with Phidias and ended with the Apollo Belvedere; and a child could travel from one to the other without danger of losing his way.

Mrs. Amyot had two fatal gifts: a capacious but inaccurate memory, and an extraordinary fluency of speech. There was nothing she did not remember-- wrongly; but her halting facts were swathed in so many layers of rhetoric that their infirmities were imperceptible to her friendly critics. Besides, she had been taught Greek by the aunt who had translated Euripides; and the mere sound of the [Greek: ais] and [Greek: ois] that she now and then not unskilfully let slip (correcting herself, of course, with a start, and indulgently mistranslating the phrase), struck awe to the hearts of ladies whose only "accomplishment" was French--if you didn't speak too quickly.

I had then but a momentary glimpse of Mrs. Amyot, but a few months later I came upon her again in the New England university town where the celebrated Irene Astarte Pratt lived on the summit of a local Parnassus, with lesser muses and college professors respectfully grouped on the lower ledges of the sacred declivity. Mrs. Amyot, who, after her husband's death, had returned to the maternal roof (even during her father's lifetime the roof had been distinctively maternal), Mrs. Amyot, thanks to her upper lip, her dimple and her Greek, was already esconced in a snug hollow of the Parnassian slope.

After the lecture was over it happened that I walked home with Mrs. Amyot. From the incensed glances of two or three learned gentlemen who were hovering on the doorstep when we emerged, I inferred that Mrs. Amyot, at that period, did not often walk home alone; but I doubt whether any of my discomfited rivals, whatever his claims to favor, was ever treated to so ravishing a mixture of shyness and self-abandonment, of sham erudition and real teeth and hair, as it was my privilege to enjoy. Even at the opening of her public career Mrs. Amyot had a tender eye for strangers, as possible links with successive centres of culture to which in due course the torch of Greek art might be handed on.

She began by telling me that she had never been so frightened in her life. She knew, of course, how dreadfully learned I was, and when, just as she was going to begin, her hostess had whispered to her that I was in the room, she had felt ready to sink through the floor. Then (with a flying dimple) she had remembered Emerson's line--wasn't it Emerson's?--that beauty is its own excuse for _seeing_, and that had made her feel a little more confident, since she was sure that no one _saw_ beauty more vividly than she--as a child she used to sit for hours gazing at an Etruscan vase on the bookcase in the library, while her sisters played with their dolls--and if _seeing_ beauty was the only excuse one needed for talking about it, why, she was sure I would make allowances and not be _too_ critical and sarcastic, especially if, as she thought probable, I had heard of her having lost her poor husband, and how she had to do it for the baby.

Being abundantly assured of my sympathy on these points, she went on to say that she had always wanted so much to consult me about her lectures. Of course, one subject wasn't enough (this view of the limitations of Greek art as a "subject" gave me a startling idea of the rate at which a successful lecturer might exhaust the universe); she must find others; she had not ventured on any as yet, but she had thought of Tennyson--didn't I _love_ Tennyson? She _worshipped_ him so that she was sure she could help others to understand him; or what did I think of a "course" on Raphael or Michelangelo--or on the heroines of Shakespeare? There were some fine steel-engravings of Raphael's Madonnas and of the Sistine ceiling in her mother's library, and she had seen Miss Cushman in several Shakespearian _roles_, so that on these subjects also she felt qualified to speak with authority.

When we reached her mother's door she begged me to come in and talk the matter over; she wanted me to see the baby--she felt as though I should understand her better if I saw the baby--and the dimple flashed through a tear.

The fear of encountering the author of "The Fall of Man," combined with the opportune recollection of a dinner engagement, made me evade this appeal with the promise of returning on the morrow. On the morrow, I left too early to redeem my promise; and for several years afterwards I saw no more of Mrs. Amyot.

My calling at that time took me at irregular intervals from one to another of our larger cities, and as Mrs. Amyot was also peripatetic it was inevitable that sooner or later we should cross each other's path. It was therefore without surprise that, one snowy afternoon in Boston, I learned from the lady with whom I chanced to be lunching that, as soon as the meal was over, I was to be taken to hear Mrs. Amyot lecture.

"On Greek art?" I suggested.

"Oh, you've heard her then? No, this is one of the series called 'Homes and Haunts of the Poets.' Last week we had Wordsworth and the Lake Poets, to-day we are to have Goethe and Weimar. She is a wonderful creature--all the women of her family are geniuses. You know, of course, that her mother was Irene Astarte Pratt, who wrote a poem on 'The Fall of Man'; N.P. Willis called her the female Milton of America. One of Mrs. Amyot's aunts has translated Eurip--"

"And is she as pretty as ever?" I irrelevantly interposed.

My hostess looked shocked. "She is excessively modest and retiring. She says it is actual suffering for her to speak in public. You know she only does it for the baby."

Punctually at the hour appointed, we took our seats in a lecture-hall full of strenuous females in ulsters. Mrs. Amyot was evidently a favorite with these austere sisters, for every corner was crowded, and as we entered a pale usher with an educated mispronunciation was setting forth to several dejected applicants the impossibility of supplying them with seats.

Our own were happily so near the front that when the curtains at the back of the platform parted, and Mrs. Amyot appeared, I was at once able to establish a comparison between the lady placidly dimpling to the applause of her public and the shrinking drawing-room orator of my earlier recollections.

Mrs. Amyot was as pretty as ever, and there was the same curious discrepancy between the freshness of her aspect and the stateness of her theme, but something was gone of the blushing unsteadiness with which she had fired her first random shots at Greek art. It was not that the shots were less uncertain, but that she now had an air of assuming that, for her purpose, the bull's-eye was everywhere, so that there was no need to be flustered in taking aim. This assurance had so facilitated the flow of her eloquence that she seemed to be performing a trick analogous to that of the conjuror who pulls hundreds of yards of white paper out of his mouth. From a large assortment of stock adjectives she chose, with unerring deftness and rapidity, the one that taste and discrimination would most surely have rejected, fitting out her subject with a whole wardrobe of slop-shop epithets irrelevant in cut and size. To the invaluable knack of not disturbing the association of ideas in her audience, she added the gift of what may be called a confidential manner--so that her fluent generalizations about Goethe and his place in literature (the lecture was, of course, manufactured out of Lewes's book) had the flavor of personal experience, of views sympathetically exchanged with her audience on the best way of knitting children's socks, or of putting up preserves for the winter. It was, I am sure, to this personal accent--the moral equivalent of her dimple--that Mrs. Amyot owed her prodigious, her irrational success. It was her art of transposing second-hand ideas into first-hand emotions that so endeared her to her feminine listeners.

To any one not in search of "documents" Mrs. Amyot's success was hardly of a kind to make her more interesting, and my curiosity flagged with the growing conviction that the "suffering" entailed on her by public speaking was at most a retrospective pang. I was sure that she had reached the point of measuring and enjoying her effects, of deliberately manipulating her public; and there must indeed have been a certain exhilaration in attaining results so considerable by means involving so little conscious effort. Mrs. Amyot's art was simply an extension of coquetry; she flirted with her audience.

In this mood of enlightened skepticism I responded but languidly to my hostess's suggestion that I should go with her that evening to see Mrs. Amyot. The aunt who had translated Euripides was at home on Saturday evenings, and one met "thoughtful" people there, my hostess explained: it was one of the intellectual centres of Boston. My mood remained distinctly resentful of any connection between Mrs. Amyot and intellectuality, and I declined to go; but the next day I met Mrs. Amyot in the street.

She stopped me reproachfully. She had heard I was in Boston; why had I not come last night? She had been told that I was at her lecture, and it had frightened her--yes, really, almost as much as years ago in Hillbridge. She never _could_ get over that stupid shyness, and the whole business was as distasteful to her as ever; but what could she do? There was the baby-- he was a big boy now, and boys were _so_ expensive! But did I really think she had improved the least little bit? And why wouldn't I come home with her now, and see the boy, and tell her frankly what I had thought of the lecture? She had plenty of flattery--people were _so_ kind, and every one knew that she did it for the baby--but what she felt the need of was criticism, severe, discriminating criticism like mine--oh, she knew that I was dreadfully discriminating!

I went home with her and saw the boy. In the early heat of her Tennyson- worship Mrs. Amyot had christened him Lancelot, and he looked it. Perhaps, however, it was his black velvet dress and the exasperating length of his yellow curls, together with the fact of his having been taught to recite Browning to visitors, that raised to fever-heat the itching of my palms in his Infant-Samuel-like presence. I have since had reason to think that he would have preferred to be called Billy, and to hunt cats with the other boys in the block: his curls and his poetry were simply another outlet for Mrs. Amyot's irrepressible coquetry.

But if Lancelot was not genuine, his mother's love for him was. It justified everything--the lectures _were_ for the baby, after all. I had not been ten minutes in the room before I was pledged to help Mrs. Amyot carry out her triumphant fraud. If she wanted to lecture on Plato she should--Plato must take his chance like the rest of us! There was no use, of course, in being "discriminating." I preserved sufficient reason to avoid that pitfall, but I suggested "subjects" and made lists of books for her with a fatuity that became more obvious as time attenuated the remembrance of her smile; I even remember thinking that some men might have cut the knot by marrying her, but I handed over Plato as a hostage and escaped by the afternoon train.

The next time I saw her was in New York, when she had become so fashionable that it was a part of the whole duty of woman to be seen at her lectures. The lady who suggested that of course I ought to go and hear Mrs. Amyot, was not very clear about anything except that she was perfectly lovely, and had had a horrid husband, and was doing it to support her boy. The subject of the discourse (I think it was on Ruskin) was clearly of minor importance, not only to my friend, but to the throng of well-dressed and absent-minded ladies who rustled in late, dropped their muffs and pocket-books, and undisguisedly lost themselves in the study of each other's apparel. They received Mrs. Amyot with warmth, but she evidently represented a social obligation like going to church, rather than any more personal interest; in fact, I suspect that every one of the ladies would have remained away, had they been sure that none of the others were coming.

Whether Mrs. Amyot was disheartened by the lack of sympathy between herself and her hearers, or whether the sport of arousing it had become a task, she certainly imparted her platitudes with less convincing warmth than of old. Her voice had the same confidential inflections, but it was like a voice reproduced by a gramophone: the real woman seemed far away. She had grown stouter without losing her dewy freshness, and her smart gown might have been taken to show either the potentialities of a settled income, or a politic concession to the taste of her hearers. As I listened I reproached myself for ever having suspected her of self-deception in saying that she took no pleasure in her work. I was sure now that she did it only for Lancelot, and judging from the size of her audience and the price of the tickets I concluded that Lancelot must be receiving a liberal education.

I was living in New York that winter, and in the rotation of dinners I found myself one evening at Mrs. Amyot's side. The dimple came out at my greeting as punctually as a cuckoo in a Swiss clock, and I detected the same automatic quality in the tone in which she made her usual pretty demand for advice. She was like a musical-box charged with popular airs. They succeeded one another with breathless rapidity, but there was a moment after each when the cylinders scraped and whizzed.

Mrs. Amyot, as I found when I called on her, was living in a sunny flat, with a sitting-room full of flowers and a tea-table that had the air of expecting visitors. She owned that she had been ridiculously successful. It was delightful, of course, on Lancelot's account. Lancelot had been sent to the best school in the country, and if things went well and people didn't tire of his silly mother he was to go to Harvard afterwards. During the next two or three years Mrs. Amyot kept her flat in New York, and radiated art and literature upon the suburbs. I saw her now and then, always stouter, better dressed, more successful and more automatic: she had become a lecturing-machine.

I went abroad for a year or two and when I came back she had disappeared. I asked several people about her, but life had closed over her. She had been last heard of as lecturing--still lecturing--but no one seemed to know when or where.

It was in Boston that I found her at last, forlornly swaying to the oscillations of an overhead strap in a crowded trolley-car. Her face had so changed that I lost myself in a startled reckoning of the time that had elapsed since our parting. She spoke to me shyly, as though aware of my hurried calculation, and conscious that in five years she ought not to have altered so much as to upset my notion of time. Then she seemed to set it down to her dress, for she nervously gathered her cloak over a gown that asked only to be concealed, and shrank into a seat behind the line of prehensile bipeds blocking the aisle of the car.

It was perhaps because she so obviously avoided me that I felt for the first time that I might be of use to her; and when she left the car I made no excuse for following her.

She said nothing of needing advice and did not ask me to walk home with her, concealing, as we talked, her transparent preoccupations under the guise of a sudden interest in all I had been doing since she had last seen me. Of what concerned her, I learned only that Lancelot was well and that for the present she was not lecturing--she was tired and her doctor had ordered her to rest. On the doorstep of a shabby house she paused and held out her hand. She had been so glad to see me and perhaps if I were in Boston again--the tired dimple, as it were, bowed me out and closed the door on the conclusion of the phrase.

Two or three weeks later, at my club in New York, I found a letter from her. In it she owned that she was troubled, that of late she had been unsuccessful, and that, if I chanced to be coming back to Boston, and could spare her a little of that invaluable advice which--. A few days later the advice was at her disposal. She told me frankly what had happened. Her public had grown tired of her. She had seen it coming on for some time, and was shrewd enough in detecting the causes. She had more rivals than formerly--younger women, she admitted, with a smile that could still afford to be generous--and then her audiences had grown more critical and consequently more exacting. Lecturing--as she understood it-- used to be simple enough. You chose your topic--Raphael, Shakespeare, Gothic Architecture, or some such big familiar "subject"--and read up about it for a week or so at the Athenaeum or the Astor Library, and then told your audience what you had read. Now, it appeared, that simple process was no longer adequate. People had tired of familiar "subjects"; it was the fashion to be interested in things that one hadn't always known about--natural selection, animal magnetism, sociology and comparative folk-lore; while, in literature, the demand had become equally difficult to meet, since Matthew Arnold had introduced the habit of studying the "influence" of one author on another. She had tried lecturing on influences, and had done very well as long as the public was satisfied with the tracing of such obvious influences as that of Turner on Ruskin, of Schiller on Goethe, of Shakespeare on English literature; but such investigations had soon lost all charm for her too-sophisticated audiences, who now demanded either that the influence or the influenced should be quite unknown, or that there should be no perceptible connection between the two. The zest of the performance lay in the measure of ingenuity with which the lecturer established a relation between two people who had probably never heard of each other, much less read each other's works. A pretty Miss Williams with red hair had, for instance, been lecturing with great success on the influence of the Rosicrucians upon the poetry of Keats, while somebody else had given a "course" on the influence of St. Thomas Aquinas upon Professor Huxley.

Mrs. Amyot, warmed by my participation in her distress, went on to say that the growing demand for evolution was what most troubled her. Her grandfather had been a pillar of the Presbyterian ministry, and the idea of her lecturing on Darwin or Herbert Spencer was deeply shocking to her mother and aunts. In one sense the family had staked its literary as well as its spiritual hopes on the literal inspiration of Genesis: what became of "The Fall of Man" in the light of modern exegesis?

The upshot of it was that she had ceased to lecture because she could no longer sell tickets enough to pay for the hire of a lecture-hall; and as for the managers, they wouldn't look at her. She had tried her luck all through the Eastern States and as far south as Washington; but it was of no use, and unless she could get hold of some new subjects--or, better still, of some new audiences--she must simply go out of the business. That would mean the failure of all she had worked for, since Lancelot would have to leave Harvard. She paused, and wept some of the unbecoming tears that spring from real grief. Lancelot, it appeared, was to be a genius. He had passed his opening examinations brilliantly; he had "literary gifts"; he had written beautiful poetry, much of which his mother had copied out, in reverentially slanting characters, in a velvet-bound volume which she drew from a locked drawer.

Lancelot's verse struck me as nothing more alarming than growing-pains; but it was not to learn this that she had summoned me. What she wanted was to be assured that he was worth working for, an assurance which I managed to convey by the simple stratagem of remarking that the poems reminded me of Swinburne--and so they did, as well as of Browning, Tennyson, Rossetti, and all the other poets who supply young authors with original inspirations.

This point being established, it remained to be decided by what means his mother was, in the French phrase, to pay herself the luxury of a poet. It was clear that this indulgence could be bought only with counterfeit coin, and that the one way of helping Mrs. Amyot was to become a party to the circulation of such currency. My fetish of intellectual integrity went down like a ninepin before the appeal of a woman no longer young and distinctly foolish, but full of those dear contradictions and irrelevancies that will always make flesh and blood prevail against a syllogism. When I took leave of Mrs. Amyot I had promised her a dozen letters to Western universities and had half pledged myself to sketch out a lecture on the reconciliation of science and religion.

In the West she achieved a success which for a year or more embittered my perusal of the morning papers. The fascination that lures the murderer back to the scene of his crime drew my eye to every paragraph celebrating Mrs. Amyot's last brilliant lecture on the influence of something upon somebody; and her own letters--she overwhelmed me with them--spared me no detail of the entertainment given in her honor by the Palimpsest Club of Omaha or of her reception at the University of Leadville. The college professors were especially kind: she assured me that she had never before met with such discriminating sympathy. I winced at the adjective, which cast a sudden light on the vast machinery of fraud that I had set in motion. All over my native land, men of hitherto unblemished integrity were conniving with me in urging their friends to go and hear Mrs. Amyot lecture on the reconciliation of science and religion! My only hope was that, somewhere among the number of my accomplices, Mrs. Amyot might find one who would marry her in the defense of his convictions.

None, apparently, resorted to such heroic measures; for about two years later I was startled by the announcement that Mrs. Amyot was lecturing in Trenton, New Jersey, on modern theosophy in the light of the Vedas. The following week she was at Newark, discussing Schopenhauer in the light of recent psychology. The week after that I was on the deck of an ocean steamer, reconsidering my share in Mrs. Amyot's triumphs with the impartiality with which one views an episode that is being left behind at the rate of twenty knots an hour. After all, I had been helping a mother to educate her son.

The next ten years of my life were spent in Europe, and when I came home the recollection of Mrs. Amyot had become as inoffensive as one of those pathetic ghosts who are said to strive in vain to make themselves visible to the living. I did not even notice the fact that I no longer heard her spoken of; she had dropped like a dead leaf from the bough of memory.

A year or two after my return I was condemned to one of the worst punishments a worker can undergo--an enforced holiday. The doctors who pronounced the inhuman sentence decreed that it should be worked out in the South, and for a whole winter I carried my cough, my thermometer and my idleness from one fashionable orange-grove to another. In the vast and melancholy sea of my disoccupation I clutched like a drowning man at any human driftwood within reach. I took a critical and depreciatory interest in the coughs, the thermometers and the idleness of my fellow-sufferers; but to the healthy, the occupied, the transient I clung with undiscriminating enthusiasm.

In no other way can I explain, as I look back on it, the importance I attached to the leisurely confidences of a new arrival with a brown beard who, tilted back at my side on a hotel veranda hung with roses, imparted to me one afternoon the simple annals of his past. There was nothing in the tale to kindle the most inflammable imagination, and though the man had a pleasant frank face and a voice differing agreeably from the shrill inflections of our fellow-lodgers, it is probable that under different conditions his discursive history of successful business ventures in a Western city would have affected me somewhat in the manner of a lullaby.

Even at the tune I was not sure I liked his agreeable voice: it had a self-importance out of keeping with the humdrum nature of his story, as though a breeze engaged in shaking out a table-cloth should have fancied itself inflating a banner. But this criticism may have been a mere mark of my own fastidiousness, for the man seemed a simple fellow, satisfied with his middling fortunes, and already (he was not much past thirty) deep-sunk in conjugal content.

He had just started on an anecdote connected with the cutting of his eldest boy's teeth, when a lady I knew, returning from her late drive, paused before us for a moment in the twilight, with the smile which is the feminine equivalent of beads to savages.

"Won't you take a ticket?" she said sweetly.

Of course I would take a ticket--but for what? I ventured to inquire.

"Oh, that's _so_ good of you--for the lecture this evening.

You needn't go, you know; we're none of us going; most of us have been through it already at Aiken and at Saint Augustine and at Palm Beach. I've given away my tickets to some new people who've just come from the North, and some of us are going to send our maids, just to fill up the room."

"And may I ask to whom you are going to pay this delicate attention?"

"Oh, I thought you knew--to poor Mrs. Amyot. She's been lecturing all over the South this winter; she's simply _haunted_ me ever since I left New York--and we had six weeks of her at Bar Harbor last summer! One has to take tickets, you know, because she's a widow and does it for her son--to pay for his education. She's so plucky and nice about it, and talks about him in such a touching unaffected way, that everybody is sorry for her, and we all simply ruin ourselves in tickets. I do hope that boy's nearly educated!"

"Mrs. Amyot? Mrs. Amyot?" I repeated. "Is she _still_ educating her son?"

"Oh, do you know about her? Has she been at it long? There's some comfort in that, for I suppose when the boy's provided for the poor thing will be able to take a rest--and give us one!"

She laughed and held out her hand.

"Here's your ticket. Did you say _tickets_--two? Oh, thanks. Of course you needn't go."

"But I mean to go. Mrs. Amyot is an old friend of mine."

"Do you really? That's awfully good of you. Perhaps I'll go too if I can persuade Charlie and the others to come. And I wonder"--in a well-directed aside--"if your friend--?"

I telegraphed her under cover of the dusk that my friend was of too recent standing to be drawn into her charitable toils, and she masked her mistake under a rattle of friendly adjurations not to be late, and to be sure to keep a seat for her, as she had quite made up her mind to go even if Charlie and the others wouldn't.

The flutter of her skirts subsided in the distance, and my neighbor, who had half turned away to light a cigar, made no effort to reopen the conversation. At length, fearing he might have overheard the allusion to himself, I ventured to ask if he were going to the lecture that evening.

"Much obliged--I have a ticket," he said abruptly.

This struck me as in such bad taste that I made no answer; and it was he who spoke next.

"Did I understand you to say that you were an old friend of Mrs. Amyot's?"

"I think I may claim to be, if it is the same Mrs. Amyot I had the pleasure of knowing many years ago. My Mrs. Amyot used to lecture too--"

"To pay for her son's education?"

"I believe so."

"Well--see you later."

He got up and walked into the house.

In the hotel drawing-room that evening there was but a meagre sprinkling of guests, among whom I saw my brown-bearded friend sitting alone on a sofa, with his head against the wall. It could not have been curiosity to see Mrs. Amyot that had impelled him to attend the performance, for it would have been impossible for him, without changing his place, to command the improvised platform at the end of the room. When I looked at him he seemed lost in contemplation of the chandelier.

The lady from whom I had bought my tickets fluttered in late, unattended by Charlie and the others, and assuring me that she would _scream_ if we had the lecture on Ibsen--she had heard it three times already that winter. A glance at the programme reassured her: it informed us (in the lecturer's own slanting hand) that Mrs. Amyot was to lecture on the Cosmogony.

After a long pause, during which the small audience coughed and moved its chairs and showed signs of regretting that it had come, the door opened, and Mrs. Amyot stepped upon the platform. Ah, poor lady!

Some one said "Hush!", the coughing and chair-shifting subsided, and she began.

It was like looking at one's self early in the morning in a

cracked mirror. I had no idea I had grown so old. As for Lancelot, he must have a beard. A beard? The word struck me, and without knowing why I glanced across the room at my bearded friend on the sofa. Oddly enough he was looking at me, with a half-defiant, half-sullen expression; and as our glances crossed, and his fell, the conviction came to me that _he was Lancelot_.

I don't remember a word of the lecture; and yet there were enough of them to have filled a good-sized dictionary. The stream of Mrs. Amyot's eloquence had become a flood: one had the despairing sense that she had sprung a leak, and that until the plumber came there was nothing to be done about it.

The plumber came at length, in the shape of a clock striking ten; my companion, with a sigh of relief, drifted away in search of Charlie and the others; the audience scattered with the precipitation of people who had discharged a duty; and, without surprise, I found the brown-bearded stranger at my elbow.

We stood alone in the bare-floored room, under the flaring chandelier.

"I think you told me this afternoon that you were an old friend of Mrs. Amyot's?" he began awkwardly.

I assented.

"Will you come in and see her?"

"Now? I shall be very glad to, if--"

"She's ready; she's expecting you," he interposed.

He offered no further explanation, and I followed him in silence. He led me down the long corridor, and pushed open the door of a sitting-room.

"Mother," he said, closing the door after we had entered, "here's the gentleman who says he used to know you."

Mrs. Amyot, who sat in an easy-chair stirring a cup of bouillon, looked up with a start. She had evidently not seen me in the audience, and her son's description had failed to convey my identity. I saw a frightened look in her eyes; then, like a frost flower on a window-pane, the dimple expanded on her wrinkled cheek, and she held out her hand.

"I'm so glad," she said, "so glad!"

She turned to her son, who stood watching us. "You must have told Lancelot all about me--you've known me so long!"

"I haven't had time to talk to your son--since I knew he was your son," I explained.

Her brow cleared. "Then you haven't had time to say anything very dreadful?" she said with a laugh.

"It is he who has been saying dreadful things," I returned, trying to fall in with her tone.

I saw my mistake. "What things?" she faltered.

"Making me feel how old I am by telling me about his children."

"My grandchildren!" she exclaimed with a blush.

"Well, if you choose to put it so."

She laughed again, vaguely, and was silent. I hesitated a moment and then put out my hand.

"I see you are tired. I shouldn't have ventured to come in at this hour if your son--"

The son stepped between us. "Yes, I asked him to come," he said to his mother, in his clear self-assertive voice. "_I_ haven't told him anything yet; but you've got to--now. That's what I brought him for."

His mother straightened herself, but I saw her eye waver.

"Lancelot--" she began.

"Mr. Amyot," I said, turning to the young man, "if your mother will let me come back to-morrow, I shall be very glad--"

He struck his hand hard against the table on which he was leaning.

"No, sir! It won't take long, but it's got to be said now."

He moved nearer to his mother, and I saw his lip twitch under his beard. After all, he was younger and less sure of himself than I had fancied.

"See here, mother," he went on, "there's something here

that's got to be cleared up, and as you say this gentleman is an old friend of yours it had better be cleared up in his presence. Maybe he can help explain it--and if he can't, it's got to be explained to _him."_

Mrs. Amyot's lips moved, but she made no sound. She glanced at me helplessly and sat down. My early inclination to thrash Lancelot was beginning to reassert itself. I took up my hat and moved toward the door.

"Mrs. Amyot is under no obligation to explain anything whatever to me," I said curtly.

"Well! She's under an obligation to me, then--to explain something in your presence." He turned to her again. "Do you know what the people in this hotel are saying? Do you know what he thinks--what they all think? That you're doing this lecturing to support me--to pay for my education! They say you go round telling them so. That's what they buy the tickets for-- they do it out of charity. Ask him if it isn't what they say--ask him if they weren't joking about it on the piazza before dinner. The others think I'm a little boy, but he's known you for years, and he must have known how old I was. _He_ must have known it wasn't to pay for my education!"

He stood before her with his hands clenched, the veins beating in his temples. She had grown very pale, and her cheeks looked hollow. When she spoke her voice had an odd click in it.

"If--if these ladies and gentlemen have been coming to my lectures out of charity, I see nothing to be ashamed of in that--" she faltered.

"If they've been coming out of charity to _me_," he retorted, "don't you see you've been making me a party to a fraud? Isn't there any shame in that?" His forehead reddened. "Mother! Can't you see the shame of letting people think I was a d--beat, who sponged on you for my keep? Let alone making us both the laughing-stock of every place you go to!"

"I never did that, Lancelot!"

"Did what?"

"Made you a laughing-stock--"

He stepped close to her and caught her wrist.

"Will you look me in the face and swear you never told people you were doing this lecturing business to support me?"

There was a long silence. He dropped her wrist and she lifted a limp handkerchief to her frightened eyes. "I did do it--to support you--to educate you"--she sobbed.

"We're not talking about what you did when I was a boy. Everybody who knows me knows I've been a grateful son. Have I ever taken a penny from you since I left college ten years ago?"

"I never said you had! How can you accuse your mother of such wickedness, Lancelot?"

"Have you never told anybody in this hotel--or anywhere else in the last ten years--that you were lecturing to support me? Answer me that!"

"How can you," she wept, "before a stranger?"

"Haven't you said such things about _me_ to strangers?" he retorted.

"Lancelot!"

"Well--answer me, then. Say you haven't, mother!" His voice broke unexpectedly and he took her hand with a gentler touch. "I'll believe anything you tell me," he said almost humbly.

She mistook his tone and raised her head with a rash clutch at dignity.

"I think you'd better ask this gentleman to excuse you first."

"No, by God, I won't!" he cried. "This gentleman says he knows all about you and I mean him to know all about me too. I don't mean that he or anybody else under this roof shall go on thinking for another twenty-four hours that a cent of their money has ever gone into my pockets since I was old enough to shift for myself. And he sha'n't leave this room till you've made that clear to him."

He stepped back as he spoke and put his shoulders against the door.

"My dear young gentleman," I said politely, "I shall leave this room exactly when I see fit to do so--and that is now. I have already told you that Mrs. Amyot owes me no explanation of her conduct."

"But I owe you an explanation of mine--you and every one who has bought a single one of her lecture tickets. Do you suppose a man who's been through what I went through while that woman was talking to you in the porch before dinner is going to hold his tongue, and not attempt to justify himself? No decent man is going to sit down under that sort of thing. It's enough to ruin his character. If you're my mother's friend, you owe it to me to hear what I've got to say."

He pulled out his handkerchief and wiped his forehead.

"Good God, mother!" he burst out suddenly, "what did you do it for? Haven't you had everything you wanted ever since I was able to pay for it? Haven't I paid you back every cent you spent on me when I was in college? Have I ever gone back on you since I was big enough to work?" He turned to me with a laugh. "I thought she did it to amuse herself--and because there was such a demand for her lectures. _Such a demand!_ That's what she always told me. When we asked her to come out and spend this winter with us in Minneapolis, she wrote back that she couldn't because she had engagements all through the south, and her manager wouldn't let her off. That's the reason why I came all the way on here to see her. We thought she was the most popular lecturer in the United States, my wife and I did! We were awfully proud of it too, I can tell you." He dropped into a chair, still laughing.

"How can you, Lancelot, how can you!" His mother, forgetful of my presence, was clinging to him with tentative caresses. "When you didn't need the money any longer I spent it all on the children--you know I did."

"Yes, on lace christening dresses and life-size rocking-horses with real manes! The kind of thing children can't do without."

"Oh, Lancelot, Lancelot--I loved them so! How can you believe such falsehoods about me?"

"What falsehoods about you?"

"That I ever told anybody such dreadful things?"

He put her back gently, keeping his eyes on hers. "Did you never tell anybody in this house that you were lecturing to support your son?"

Her hands dropped from his shoulders and she flashed round on me in sudden anger.

"I know what I think of people who call themselves friends and who come between a mother and her son!"

"Oh, mother, mother!" he groaned.

I went up to him and laid my hand on his shoulder.

"My dear man," I said, "don't you see the uselessness of prolonging this?"

"Yes, I do," he answered abruptly; and before I could forestall his movement he rose and walked out of the room.

There was a long silence, measured by the lessening reverberations of his footsteps down the wooden floor of the corridor.

When they ceased I approached Mrs. Amyot, who had sunk into her chair. I held out my hand and she took it without a trace of resentment on her ravaged face.

"I sent his wife a seal-skin jacket at Christmas!" she said, with the tears running down her cheeks.

The Pretext

I

MRS. RANSOM, WHEN THE FRONT DOOR had closed on her visitor, passed with a spring from the drawing-room to the narrow hall, and thence up the narrow stairs to her bedroom.

Though slender, and still light of foot, she did not always move so quickly: hitherto, in her life, there had not been much to hurry for, save the recurring domestic tasks that compel haste without fostering elasticity; but some impetus of youth revived, communicated to her by her talk with Guy Dawnish, now found expression in her girlish flight upstairs, her girlish impatience to bolt herself into her room with her throbs and her blushes.

Her blushes? Was she really blushing?

She approached the cramped eagle-topped mirror above her plain prim dressing-table: just such a meagre concession to the weakness of the flesh as every old-fashioned house in Wentworth counted among its relics. The face reflected in this unflattering surface--for even the mirrors of Wentworth erred on the side of depreciation--did not seem, at first sight, a suitable theatre for the display of the tenderer emotions, and its owner blushed more deeply as the fact was forced upon her.

Her fair hair had grown too thin--it no longer quite hid the blue veins in her candid forehead--a forehead that one seemed to see turned toward professorial desks, in large bare halls where a snowy winter light fell uncompromisingly on rows of "thoughtful women." Her mouth was thin, too, and a little strained; her lips were too pale; and there were lines in the corners of her eyes. It was a face which had grown middle-aged while it waited for the joys of youth.

Well--but if she could still blush? Instinctively she drew back a little, so that her scrutiny became less microscopic, and the pretty lingering pink threw a veil over her pallor, the hollows in her temples, the faint wrinkles of inexperience about her lips and eyes. How a little colour helped! It made her eyes so deep and shining. She saw now why bad women rouged. . . . Her redness deepened at the thought.

But suddenly she noticed for the first time that the collar of her dress was cut too low. It showed the shrunken lines of the throat. She rummaged feverishly in a tidy scentless drawer, and snatching out a bit of black velvet, bound it about her neck. Yes--that was better. It gave her the relief she needed. Relief--contrast--that was it! She had never had any, either in her appearance or in her setting. She was as flat as the pattern of the wall-paper--and so was her life. And all the people about her had the same look. Wentworth was the kind of place where husbands and wives gradually grew to resemble each other--one or two of her friends, she remembered, had told her lately that she and Ransom were beginning to look alike. . . .

But why had she always, so tamely, allowed her aspect to conform to her situation? Perhaps a gayer exterior would have provoked a brighter fate. Even now--she turned back to the glass, loosened the tight strands of hair above her brow, ran the fine end of the comb under them with a rapid frizzing motion, and then disposed them, more lightly and amply, above her eager face. Yes--it was really better; it made a difference. She smiled at herself with a timid coquetry, and her lips seemed rosier as she smiled. Then she laid down the comb and the smile faded. It made a difference, certainly--but was it right to try to make one's hair look thicker and wavier than it really was? Between that and rouging the ethical line seemed almost impalpable, and the spectre of her rigid New England ancestry rose reprovingly before her. She was sure that none of her grandmothers had ever simulated a curl or encouraged a blush. A blush, indeed! What had any of them ever had to blush for in all their frozen lives? And what, in Heaven's name, had she? She sat down in the stiff mahogany rocking-chair beside her work-table and tried to collect herself. From childhood she had been taught to "collect herself"--but never before had her small sensations and aspirations been so widely scattered, diffused over so vague and uncharted an expanse. Hitherto they had lain in neatly sorted and easily accessible bundles on the high shelves of a perfectly ordered moral consciousness. And now--now that for the first time they _needed_ collecting--now that the little winged and scattered bits of self were dancing madly down the vagrant winds of fancy, she knew no spell to call them to the fold again. The best way, no doubt--if only her bewilderment permitted--was to go back to the beginning--the beginning, at least, of to-day's visit--to recapitulate, word for word and look for look. . . .

She clasped her hands on the arms of the chair, checked its swaying with a firm thrust of her foot, and fixed her eyes upon the inward vision. . . .

To begin with, what had made to-day's visit so different from the others? It became suddenly vivid to her that there had been many, almost daily, others, since Guy Dawnish's coming to Wentworth. Even the previous winter--the winter of his arrival from England--his visits had been numerous enough to make Wentworth aware that--very naturally--Mrs. Ransom was "looking after" the stray young Englishman committed to her husband's care by an eminent Q. C. whom the Ransoms had known on one of their brief London visits, and with whom Ransom had since maintained professional relations. All this was in the natural order of things, as sanctioned by the social code of Wentworth. Every one was kind to Guy Dawnish--some rather importunately so, as Margaret Ransom had smiled to observe--but it was recognized as fitting that she should be kindest, since he was in a sense her property, since his people in England, by profusely acknowledging her kindness, had given it the domestic sanction without which, to Wentworth, any social relation between the sexes remained unhallowed and to be viewed askance. Yes! And even this second winter, when the visits had become so much more frequent, so admitted a part of the day's routine, there had not been, from any one, a hint of surprise or of conjecture. . . .

Mrs. Ransom smiled with a faint bitterness. She was protected by her age, no doubt--her age and her past, and the image her mirror gave back to her. . . .

Her door-handle turned suddenly, and the bolt's resistance was met by an impatient knock.

"Margaret!"

She started up, her brightness fading, and unbolted the door to admit her husband.

"Why are you locked in? Why, you're not dressed yet!" he exclaimed.

It was possible for Ransom to reach his dressing-room by a slight circuit through the passage; but it was characteristic of the relentless domesticity of their relation that he chose, as a matter of course, the directer way through his wife's bedroom. She had never before been disturbed by this practice, which she accepted as inevitable, but had merely adapted her own habits to it, delaying her hasty toilet till he was safely in his room, or completing it before she heard his step on the stair; since a scrupulous traditional prudery had miraculously survived this massacre of all the privacies.

"Oh, I shan't dress this evening--I shall just have some tea in the library after you've gone," she answered absently. "Your things are laid out," she added, rousing herself.

He looked surprised. "The dinner's at seven. I suppose the speeches will begin at nine. I thought you were coming to hear them."

She wavered. "I don't know. I think not. Mrs. Sperry's ill, and I've no one else to go with."

He glanced at his watch. "Why not get hold of Dawnish? Wasn't he here just now? Why didn't you ask him?"

She turned toward her dressing-table, and straightened the comb and brush with a nervous hand. Her husband had given her, that morning, two tickets for the ladies' gallery in Hamblin Hall, where the great public dinner of the evening was to take place--a banquet offered by the faculty of Wentworth to visitors of academic eminence--and she had meant to ask Dawnish to go with her: it had seemed the most natural thing to do, till the end of his visit came, and then, after all, she had not spoken. . . .

"It's too late now," she murmured, bending over her pin cushion.

"Too late? Not if you telephone him."

Her husband came toward her, and she turned quickly to face him, lest he should suspect her of trying to avoid his eye. To what duplicity was she already committed!

Ransom laid a friendly hand on her arm: "Come along, Margaret. You know I speak for the bar." She was aware, in his voice, of a little note of surprise at his having to remind her of this.

"Oh, yes. I meant to go, of course--"

"Well, then--" He opened his dressing-room door, and caught a glimpse of the retreating house-maid's skirt. "Here's Maria now. Maria! Call up Mr. Dawnish--at Mrs. Creswell's, you know. Tell him Mrs. Ransom wants him to go with her to hear the speeches this evening--the _speeches_, you understand?--and he's to call for her at a quarter before nine."

Margaret heard the Irish "Yessir" on the stairs, and stood motionless, while her husband added loudly: "And bring me some towels when you come up." Then he turned back into his wife's room.

"Why, it would be a thousand pities for Guy to miss this. He's so interested in the way we do things over here--and I don't know that he's ever heard me speak in public." Again the slight note of fatuity! Was it possible that Ransom was a fatuous man?

He paused in front of her, his short-sighted unobservant glance concentrating itself unexpectedly on her face.

"You're not going like that, are you?" he asked, with glaring eye-glasses.

"Like what?" she faltered, lifting a conscious hand to the velvet at her throat.

"With your hair in such a fearful mess. Have you been shampooing it? You look like the Brant girl at the end of a tennis-match."

The Brant girl was their horror--the horror of all right-thinking Wentworth; a laced, whale-boned, frizzle-headed, high-heeled daughter of iniquity, who came--from New York, of course--on long, disturbing, tumultuous visits to a Wentworth aunt, working havoc among the freshmen, and leaving, when she departed, an angry wake of criticism that ruffled the social waters for weeks. _She_, too, had tried her hand at Guy--with ludicrous unsuccess. And now, to be compared to her--to be accused of looking "New Yorky!" Ah, there are times when husbands are obtuse; and Ransom, as he stood there, thick and yet juiceless, in his dry legal middle age, with his wiry dust-coloured beard, and his perpetual _pince-nez_, seemed to his wife a sudden embodiment of this traditional attribute. Not that she had ever fancied herself, poor soul, a "_ femme incomprise_." She had, on the contrary, prided herself on being understood by her husband, almost as much as on her own complete comprehension of him. Wentworth laid a good deal of stress on "motives"; and Margaret Ransom and her husband had dwelt in a complete community of motive. It had been the proudest day of her life when, without consulting her, he had refused an offer of partnership in an eminent New York firm because he preferred the distinction of practising in Wentworth, of being known as the legal representative of the University. Wentworth, in fact, had always been the bond between the two; they were united in their veneration for that estimable seat of learning, and in their modest yet vivid consciousness of possessing its tone. The Wentworth "tone" is unmistakable: it permeates every part of the social economy, from the _coiffure_ of the ladies to the preparation of the food. It has its sumptuary laws as well as its curriculum of learning. It sits in judgment not only on its own townsmen but on the rest of the world--enlightening, criticising, ostracizing a heedless universe--and non-conformity to Wentworth standards involves obliteration from Wentworth's consciousness.

In a world without traditions, without reverence, without stability, such little expiring centres of prejudice and precedent make an irresistible appeal to those instincts for which a democracy has neglected to provide. Wentworth, with its "tone," its backward references, its inflexible aversions and condemnations, its hard moral outline preserved intact against a whirling background of experiment, had been all the poetry and history of Margaret Ransom's life. Yes, what she had really esteemed in her husband was the fact of his being so intense an embodiment of Wentworth; so long and closely identified, for instance, with its legal affairs, that he was almost a part of its university existence, that of course, at a college banquet, he would inevitably speak for the bar!

It was wonderful of how much consequence all this had seemed till now. . . .

II

When, punctually at ten minutes to seven, her husband had emerged from the house, Margaret Ransom remained seated in her bedroom, addressing herself anew to the difficult process of self-collection. As an aid to this endeavour, she bent forward and looked out of the window, following Ransom's figure as it receded down the elm-shaded street. He moved almost alone between the prim flowerless grass-plots, the white porches, the protrusion of irrelevant shingled gables, which stamped the empty street as part of an American college town. She had always been proud of living in Hill Street, where the university people congregated, proud to associate her husband's retreating back, as he walked daily to his office, with backs literary and pedagogic, backs of which it was whispered, for the edification of duly-impressed visitors: "Wait till that old boy turns--that's so-and-so."

This had been her world, a world destitute of personal experience, but filled with a rich sense of privilege and distinction, of being not as those millions were who, denied the inestimable advantage of living at Wentworth, pursued elsewhere careers foredoomed to futility by that very fact.

And now--!

She rose and turned to her work-table where she had dropped, on entering, the handful of photographs that Guy Dawnish had left with her. While he sat so close, pointing out and explaining, she had hardly taken in the details; but now, on the full tones of his low young voice, they came back with redoubled distinctness. This was Guise Abbey, his uncle's place in Wiltshire, where, under his grandfather's rule, Guy's own boyhood had been spent: a long gabled Jacobean facade, many-chimneyed, ivy-draped, overhung (she felt sure) by the boughs of a venerable rookery. And in this other picture--the walled garden at Guise--that was his uncle, Lord Askern, a hale gouty-looking figure, planted robustly on the terrace, a gun on his shoulder and a couple of setters at his feet. And here was the river below the park, with Guy "punting" a girl in a flapping hat--how Margaret hated the flap that hid the girl's face! And here was the tennis-court, with Guy among a jolly cross-legged group of youths in flannels, and pretty girls about the tea-table under the big lime: in the centre the curate handing bread and butter, and in the middle distance a footman approaching with more cups.

Margaret raised this picture closer to her eyes, puzzling, in the diminished light, over the face of the girl nearest to Guy Dawnish--bent above him in profile, while he laughingly lifted his head. No hat hid this profile, which stood out clearly against the foliage behind it.

"And who is that handsome girl?" Margaret had said,

detaining the photograph as he pushed it aside, and struck by the fact that, of the whole group, he had left only this member unnamed.

"Oh, only Gwendolen Matcher--I've always known her--. Look at this: the almshouses at Guise. Aren't they jolly?"

And then--without her having had the courage to ask if the girl in the punt were also Gwendolen Matcher--they passed on to photographs of his rooms at Oxford, of a cousin's studio in London--one of Lord Askern's grandsons was "artistic"--of the rose-hung cottage in Wales to which, on the old Earl's death, his daughter-in-law, Guy's mother, had retired.

Every one of the photographs opened a window on the life Margaret had been trying to picture since she had known him--a life so rich, so romantic, so packed--in the mere casual vocabulary of daily life--with historic reference and poetic allusion, that she felt almost oppressed by this distant whiff of its air. The very words he used fascinated and bewildered her. He seemed to have been born into all sorts of connections, political, historical, official, that made the Ransom situation at Wentworth as featureless as the top shelf of a dark closet. Some one in the family had "asked for the Chiltern Hundreds"--one uncle was an Elder Brother of the Trinity House--some one else was the Master of a College--some one was in command at Devonport--the Army, the Navy, the House of Commons, the House of Lords, the most venerable seats of learning, were all woven into the dense background of this young man's light unconscious talk. For the unconsciousness was unmistakable. Margaret was not without experience of the transatlantic visitor who sounds loud names and evokes reverberating connections. The poetry of Guy Dawnish's situation lay in the fact that it was so completely a part of early associations and accepted facts. Life was like that in England--in Wentworth of course (where he had been sent, through his uncle's influence, for two years' training in the neighbouring electrical works at Smedden)--in Wentworth, though "immensely jolly," it was different. The fact that he was qualifying to be an electrical engineer--with the hope of a secretaryship at the London end of the great Smedden Company--that, at best, he was returning home to a life of industrial "grind," this fact, though avowedly a bore, did not disconnect him from that brilliant pinnacled past, that many-faceted life in which the brightest episodes of the whole body of English fiction seemed collectively reflected. Of course he would have to work--younger sons' sons almost always had to--but his uncle Askern (like Wentworth) was "immensely jolly," and Guise always open to him, and his other uncle, the Master, a capital old boy too--and in town he could always put up with his clever aunt, Lady Caroline Duckett, who had made a "beastly marriage" and was horribly poor, but who knew everybody jolly and amusing, and had always been particularly kind to him.

It was not--and Margaret had not, even in her own thoughts, to defend herself from the imputation--it was not what Wentworth would have called the "material side" of her friend's situation that captivated her. She was austerely proof against such appeals: her enthusiasms were all of the imaginative order. What subjugated her was the unexampled prodigality with which he poured for her the same draught of tradition of which Wentworth held out its little teacupful. He besieged her with a million Wentworths in one--saying, as it were: "All these are mine for the asking--and I choose you instead!"

For this, she told herself somewhat dizzily, was what it came to--the summing-up toward which her conscientious efforts at self-collection had been gradually pushing her: with all this in reach, Guy Dawnish was leaving Wentworth reluctantly.

"I _was_ a bit lonely here at first--but _now!_" And again: "It will be jolly, of course, to see them all again--but there are some things one doesn't easily give up. . . ."

If he had known only Wentworth, it would have been wonderful enough that he should have chosen her out of all Wentworth--but to have known that other life, and to set her in the balance against it--poor Margaret Ransom, in whom, at the moment, nothing seemed of weight but her years! Ah, it might well produce, in nerves and brain, and poor unpractised pulses, a flushed tumult of sensation, the rush of a great wave of life, under which memory struggled in vain to reassert itself, to particularize again just what his last words--the very last--had been. . . .

When consciousness emerged, quivering, from this retrospective assault, it pushed Margaret Ransom--feeling herself a mere leaf in the blast--toward the writing-table from which her innocent and voluminous correspondence habitually flowed. She had a letter to write now--much shorter but more difficult than any she had ever been called on to indite.

"Dear Mr. Dawnish," she began, "since telephoning you just now I have decided not--"

Maria's voice, at the door, announced that tea was in the library: "And I s'pose it's the brown silk you'll wear to the speaking?"

In the usual order of the Ransom existence, its mistress's toilet was performed unassisted; and the mere enquiry--at once friendly and deferential--projected, for Margaret, a strong light on the importance of the occasion. That she should answer: "But I am not going," when the going was so manifestly part of a household solemnity about which the thoughts below stairs fluttered in proud participation; that in face of such participation she should utter a word implying indifference or hesitation--nay, revealing herself the transposed, uprooted thing she had been on the verge of becoming; to do this was--well! infinitely harder than to perform the alternative act of tearing up the sheet of note-paper under her reluctant pen.

Yes, she said, she would wear the brown silk. . . .

III

All the heat and glare from the long illuminated table, about which the fumes of many courses still hung in a savoury fog, seemed to surge up to the ladies' gallery, and concentrate themselves in the burning cheeks of a slender figure withdrawn behind the projection of a pillar.

It never occurred to Margaret Ransom that she was sitting in the shade. She supposed that the full light of the chandeliers was beating on her face--and there were moments when it seemed as though all the heads about the great horse-shoe below, bald, shaggy, sleek, close-thatched, or thinly latticed, were equipped with an additional pair of eyes, set at an angle which enabled them to rake her face as relentlessly as the electric burners.

In the lull after a speech, the gallery was fluttering with the rustle of programmes consulted, and Mrs. Sheff (the Brant girl's aunt) leaned forward to say enthusiastically: "And now we're to hear Mr. Ransom!"

A louder buzz rose from the table, and the heads (without relaxing their upward vigilance) seemed to merge, and flow together, like an attentive flood, toward the upper end of the horse-shoe, where all the threads of Margaret Ransom's consciousness were suddenly drawn into what seemed a small speck, no more--a black speck that rose, hung in air, dissolved into gyrating gestures, became distended, enormous, preponderant--became her husband "speaking."

"It's the heat--" Margaret gasped, pressing her handkerchief to her whitening lips, and finding just strength enough left to push back farther into the shadow.

She felt a touch on her arm. "It _is_ horrible--shall we go?" a voice suggested; and, "Yes, yes, let us go," she whispered, feeling, with a great throb of relief, _that_ to be the only possible, the only conceivable, solution. To sit and listen to her husband _now_--how could she ever have thought she could survive it? Luckily, under the lingering hubbub from below, his opening words were inaudible, and she had only to run the gauntlet of sympathetic feminine glances, shot after her between waving fans and programmes, as, guided by Guy Dawnish, she managed to reach the door. It was really so hot that even Mrs. Sheff was not much surprised--till long afterward. . . .

The winding staircase was empty, half dark and blessedly silent. In a committee room below Dawnish found the inevitable water jug, and filled a glass for her, while she leaned back, confronted only by a frowning college President in an emblazoned frame. The academic frown descended on her like an anathema when she rose and followed her companion out of the building.

Hamblin Hall stands at the end of the long green "Campus" with its sextuple line of elms--the boast and the singularity of Wentworth. A pale spring moon, rising above the dome of the University library at the opposite end of the elm-walk, diffused a pearly mildness in the sky, melted to thin haze the shadows of the trees, and turned to golden yellow the lights of the college windows. Against this soft suffusion of light the Library cupola assumed a Bramantesque grace, the white steeple of the congregational church became a campanile topped by a winged spirit, and the scant porticoes of the older halls the colonnades of classic temples.

"This is better--" Dawnish said, as they passed down the steps and under the shadow of the elms.

They moved on a little way in silence before he began again: "You're too tired to walk. Let us sit down a few minutes."

Her feet, in truth, were leaden, and not far off a group of park benches, encircling the pedestal of a patriot in bronze, invited them to rest. But Dawnish was guiding her toward a lateral path which bent, through shrubberies, toward a strip of turf between two of the buildings.

"It will be cooler by the river," he said, moving on without waiting for a possible protest. None came: it seemed easier, for the moment, to let herself be led without any conventional feint of resistance. And besides, there was nothing wrong about _this_--the wrong would have been in sitting up there in the glare, pretending to listen to her husband, a dutiful wife among her kind. . . .

The path descended, as both knew, to the chosen, the inimitable spot of Wentworth: that fugitive curve of the river, where, before hurrying on to glut the brutal industries of South Wentworth and Smedden, it simulated for a few hundred yards the leisurely pace of an ancient university stream, with willows on its banks and a stretch of turf extending from the grounds of Hamblin Hall to the boat houses at the farther bend. Here too were benches, beneath the willows, and so close to the river that the voice of its gliding softened and filled out the reverberating silence between Margaret and her companion, and made her feel that she knew why he had brought her there.

"Do you feel better?" he asked gently as he sat down beside her.

"Oh, yes. I only needed a little air."

"I'm so glad you did. Of course the speeches were tremendously interesting--but I prefer this. What a good night!"

"Yes."

There was a pause, which now, after all, the soothing accompaniment of the river seemed hardly sufficient to fill.

"I wonder what time it is. I ought to be going home," Margaret began at length.

"Oh, it's not late. They'll be at it for hours in there--yet."

She made a faint inarticulate sound. She wanted to say: "No--Robert's speech was to be the last--" but she could not bring herself to pronounce Ransom's name, and at the moment no other way of refuting her companion's statement occurred to her.

The young man leaned back luxuriously, reassured by her silence.

"You see it's my last chance--and I want to make the most of it."

"Your last chance?" How stupid of her to repeat his words on that cooing note of interrogation! It was just such a lead as the Brant girl might have given him.

"To be with you--like this. I haven't had so many. And there's less than a week left."

She attempted to laugh. "Perhaps it will sound longer if you call it five days."

The flatness of that, again! And she knew there were people who called her intelligent. Fortunately he did not seem to notice it; but her laugh continued to sound in her own ears--the coquettish chirp of middle age! She decided that if he spoke again--if he _said anything_--she would make no farther effort at evasion: she would take it directly, seriously, frankly--she would not be doubly disloyal.

"Besides," he continued, throwing his arm along the back of the bench, and turning toward her so that his face was like a dusky bas-relief with a silver rim--"besides, there's something I've been wanting to tell you."

The sound of the river seemed to cease altogether: the whole world became silent.

Margaret had trusted her inspiration farther than it appeared likely to carry her. Again she could think of nothing happier than to repeat, on the same witless note of interrogation: "To tell me?"

"You only."

The constraint, the difficulty, seemed to be on his side now: she divined it by the renewed shifting of his attitude--he was capable, usually, of such fine intervals of immobility--and by a confusion in his utterance that set her own voice throbbing in her throat.

"You've been so perfect to me," he began again. "It's not my fault if you've made me feel that you would understand everything--make allowances for everything--see just how a man may have held out, and fought against a thing--as long as he had the strength. . . . This may be my only chance; and I can't go away without telling you."

He had turned from her now, and was staring at the river, so that his profile was projected against the moonlight in all its beautiful young dejection.

There was a slight pause, as though he waited for her to speak; then she leaned forward and laid her hand on his.

"If I have really been--if I have done for you even the least part of what you say . . . what you imagine . . . will you do for me, now, just one thing in return?"

He sat motionless, as if fearing to frighten away the shy touch on his hand, and she left it there, conscious of her gesture only as part of the high ritual of their farewell.

"What do you want me to do?" he asked in a low tone.

"_ Not_ to tell me!" she breathed on a deep note of entreaty.

"_ Not_ to tell you--?"

"Anything--_anything_--just to leave our . . . our friendship . . . as it has been--as--as a painter, if a friend asked him, might leave a picture--not quite finished, perhaps . . . but all the more exquisite. . . ."

She felt the hand under hers slip away, recover itself, and seek her own, which had flashed out of reach in the same instant--felt the start that swept him round on her as if he had been caught and turned about by the shoulders.

"You--_you_--?" he stammered, in a strange voice full of fear and tenderness; but she held fast, so centred in her inexorable resolve that she was hardly conscious of the effect her words might be producing.

"Don't you see," she hurried on, "don't you _feel_ how much safer it is--yes, I'm willing to put it so!--how much safer to leave everything undisturbed . . . just as . . . as it has grown of itself . . . without trying to say: 'It's this or that' . . . ? It's what we each choose to call it to ourselves, after all, isn't it? Don't let us try to find a name that . . . that we should both agree upon . . . we probably shouldn't succeed." She laughed abruptly. "And ghosts vanish when one names them!" she ended with a break in her voice.

When she ceased her heart was beating so violently that there was a rush in her ears like the noise of the river after rain, and she did not immediately make out what he was answering. But as she recovered her lucidity she said to herself that, whatever he was saying, she must not hear it; and she began to speak again, half playfully, half appealingly, with an eloquence of entreaty, an ingenuity in argument, of which she had never dreamed herself capable. And then, suddenly, strangling hands seemed to reach up from her heart to her throat, and she had to stop.

Her companion remained motionless. He had not tried to regain her hand, and his eyes were away from her, on the river. But his nearness had become something formidable and exquisite--something she had never before imagined. A flush of guilt swept over her--vague reminiscences of French novels and of opera plots. This was what such women felt, then . . . this was "shame." . . . Phrases of the newspaper and the pulpit danced before her. . . . She dared not speak, and his silence began to frighten her. Had ever a heart beat so wildly before in Wentworth?

He turned at last, and taking her two hands, quite simply, kissed them one after the other.

"I shall never forget--" he said in a confused voice, unlike his own.

A return of strength enabled her to rise, and even to let her eyes meet his for a moment.

"Thank you," she said, simply also.

She turned away from the bench, regaining the path that led back to the college buildings, and he walked beside her in silence. When they reached the elm walk it was dotted with dispersing groups. The "speaking" was over, and Hamblin Hall had poured its audience out into the moonlight. Margaret felt a rush of relief, followed by a receding wave of regret. She had the distinct sensation that her hour--her one hour--was over.

One of the groups just ahead broke up as they approached, and projected Ransom's solid bulk against the moonlight.

"My husband," she said, hastening forward; and she never afterward forgot the look of his back--heavy, round-shouldered, yet a little pompous--in a badly fitting overcoat that stood out at the neck and hid his collar. She had never before noticed how he dressed.

IV

They met again, inevitably, before Dawnish left; but the thing she feared did not happen--he did not try to see her alone.

It even became clear to her, in looking back, that he had deliberately avoided doing so; and this seemed merely an added proof of his "understanding," of that deep undefinable communion that set them alone in an empty world, as if on a peak above the clouds.

The five days passed in a flash; and when the last one came, it brought to Margaret Ransom an hour of weakness, of profound disorganization, when old barriers fell, old convictions faded--when to be alone with him for a moment became, after all, the one craving of her heart. She knew he was coming that afternoon to say "good-by"--and she knew also that Ransom was to be away at South Wentworth. She waited alone in her pale little drawing- room, with its scant kakemonos, its one or two chilly reproductions from the antique, its slippery Chippendale chairs. At length the bell rang, and her world became a rosy blur--through which she presently discerned the austere form of Mrs. Sperry, wife of the Professor of palaeontology, who had come to talk over with her the next winter's programme for the Higher Thought Club. They debated the question for an hour, and when Mrs. Sperry departed Margaret had a confused impression that the course was to deal with the influence of the First Crusade on the development of European architecture--but the sentient part of her knew only that Dawnish had not come.

He "bobbed in," as he would have put it, after dinner--having, it appeared, run across Ransom early in the day, and learned that the latter would be absent till evening. Margaret was in the study with her husband when the door opened and Dawnish stood there. Ransom--who had not had time to dress--was seated at his desk, a pile of shabby law books at his elbow, the light from a hanging lamp falling on his grayish stubble of hair, his sallow forehead and spectacled eyes. Dawnish, towering higher than usual against the shadows of the room, and refined by his unusual pallor, hung a moment on the threshold, then came in, explaining himself profusely--laughing, accepting a cigar, letting Ransom push an arm-chair forward--a Dawnish she had never seen, ill at ease, ejaculatory, yet somehow more mature, more obscurely in command of himself.

Margaret drew back, seating herself in the shade, in such a way that she saw her husband's head first, and beyond it their visitor's, relieved against the dusk of the book shelves. Her heart was still--she felt no throbbing in her throat or temples: all her life seemed concentrated in the hand that lay on her knee, the hand he would touch when they said good-by.

Afterward her heart rang all the changes, and there was a mood in which she reproached herself for cowardice--for having deliberately missed her one moment with him, the moment in which she might have sounded the depths of life, for joy or anguish. But that mood was fleeting and infrequent. In quieter hours she blushed for it--she even trembled to think that he might have guessed such a regret in her. It seemed to convict her of a lack of fineness that he should have had, in his youth and his power, a tenderer, surer sense of the peril of a rash touch--should have handled the case so much more delicately.

At first her days were fire and the nights long solemn vigils. Her thoughts were no longer vulgarized and defaced by any notion of "guilt," of mental disloyalty. She was ashamed now of her shame. What had happened was as much outside the sphere of her marriage as some transaction in a star. It had simply given her a secret life of incommunicable joys, as if all the wasted springs of her youth had been stored in some hidden pool, and she could return there now to bathe in them.

After that there came a phase of loneliness, through which the life about her loomed phantasmal and remote. She thought the dead must feel thus, repeating the vain gestures of the living beside some Stygian shore. She wondered if any other woman had lived to whom _nothing had ever happened?_ And then his first letter came. . . .

It was a charming letter--a perfect letter. The little touch of awkwardness and constraint under its boyish spontaneity told her more than whole pages of eloquence. He spoke of their friendship--of their good days together. . . . Ransom, chancing to come in while she read, noticed the foreign stamps; and she was able to hand him the letter, saying gaily: "There's a message for you," and knowing all the while that _her_ message was safe in her heart.

On the days when the letters came the outlines of things grew indistinct, and she could never afterward remember what she had done or how the business of life had been carried on. It was always a surprise when she found dinner on the table as usual, and Ransom seated opposite to her, running over the evening paper.

But though Dawnish continued to write, with all the English loyalty to the outward observances of friendship, his communications came only at intervals of several weeks, and between them she had time to repossess herself, to regain some sort of normal contact with life. And the customary, the recurring, gradually reclaimed her, the net of habit tightened again--her daily life became real, and her one momentary escape from it an exquisite illusion. Not that she ceased to believe in the miracle that had befallen her: she still treasured the reality of her one moment beside the river.

What reason was there for doubting it? She could hear the ring of truth in young Dawnish's voice: "It's not my fault if you've made me feel that you would understand everything. . . ." No! she believed in her miracle, and the belief sweetened and illumined her life; but she came to see that what was for her the transformation of her whole being might well have been, for her companion, a mere passing explosion of gratitude, of boyish good-fellowship touched with the pang of leave-taking. She even reached the point of telling herself that it was "better so": this view of the episode so defended it from the alternating extremes of self-reproach and derision, so enshrined it in a pale immortality to which she could make her secret pilgrimages without reproach.

For a long time she had not been able to pass by the bench under the willows--she even avoided the elm walk till autumn had stripped its branches. But every day, now, she noted a step toward recovery; and at last a day came when, walking along the river, she said to herself, as she approached the bench: "I used not to be able to pass here without thinking of him; _and now I am not thinking of him at all!_"

This seemed such convincing proof of her recovery that she began, as spring returned, to permit herself, now and then, a quiet session on the bench--a dedicated hour from which she went back fortified to her task.

She had not heard from her friend for six weeks or more--the intervals between his letters were growing longer. But that was "best" too, and she was not anxious, for she knew he had obtained the post he had been preparing for, and that his active life in London had begun. The thought reminded her, one mild March day, that in leaving the house she had thrust in her reticule a letter from a Wentworth friend who was abroad on a holiday. The envelope bore the London post mark, a fact showing that the lady's face was turned toward home. Margaret seated herself on her bench, and drawing out the letter began to read it.

The London described was that of shops and museums--as remote as possible from the setting of Guy Dawnish's existence. But suddenly Margaret's eye fell on his name, and the page began to tremble in her hands.

"I heard such a funny thing yesterday about your friend Mr. Dawnish. We went to a tea at Professor Bunce's (I do wish you knew the Bunces--their atmosphere is so _uplifting_), and there I met that Miss Bruce-Pringle who came out last year to take a course in histology at the Annex. Of course she asked about you and Mr. Ransom, and then she told me she had just seen Mr. Dawnish's aunt--the clever one he was always talking about, Lady Caroline something--and that they were all in a dreadful state about him. I wonder if you knew he was engaged when he went to America? He never mentioned it to _us_. She said it was not a positive engagement, but an understanding with a girl he has always been devoted to, who lives near their place in Wiltshire; and both families expected the marriage to take place as soon as he got back. It seems the girl is an heiress (you know _how low_ the English ideals are compared with ours), and Miss Bruce-Pringle said his relations were perfectly delighted at his 'being provided for,' as she called it. Well, when he got back he asked the girl to release him; and she and her family were furious, and so were his people; but he holds out, and won't marry her, and won't give a reason, except that he has 'formed an unfortunate attachment.' Did you ever hear anything so peculiar? His aunt, who is quite wild about it, says it must have happened at Wentworth, because he didn't go anywhere else in America. Do you suppose it _could_ have been the Brant girl? But why 'unfortunate' when everybody knows she would have jumped at him?"

Margaret folded the letter and looked out across the river. It was not the same river, but a mystic current shot with moonlight. The bare willows wove a leafy veil above her head, and beside her she felt the nearness of youth and tempestuous tenderness. It had all happened just here, on this very seat by the river--it had come to her, and passed her by, and she had not held out a hand to detain it. . . .

Well! Was it not, by that very abstention, made more deeply and ineffaceably hers? She could argue thus while she had thought the episode, on his side, a mere transient effect of propinquity; but now that she knew it had altered the whole course of his life, now that it took on substance and reality, asserted a separate existence outside of her own troubled consciousness--now it seemed almost cowardly to have missed her share in it.

She walked home in a dream. Now and then, when she passed an acquaintance, she wondered if the pain and glory were written on her face. But Mrs. Sperry, who stopped her at the corner of Maverick Street to say a word about the next meeting of the Higher Thought Club, seemed to remark no change in her.

When she reached home Ransom had not yet returned from the office, and she went straight to the library to tidy his writing-table. It was part of her daily duty to bring order out of the chaos of his papers, and of late she had fastened on such small recurring tasks as some one falling over a precipice might snatch at the weak bushes in its clefts.

When she had sorted the letters she took up some pamphlets and newspapers, glancing over them to see if they were to be kept. Among the papers was a page torn from a London _Times_ of the previous month. Her eye ran down its columns and suddenly a paragraph flamed out.

"We are requested to state that the marriage arranged between Mr. Guy Dawnish, son of the late Colonel the Hon. Roderick Dawnish, of Malby, Wilts, and Gwendolen, daughter of Samuel Matcher, Esq. of Armingham Towers, Wilts, will not take place."

Margaret dropped the paper and sat down, hiding her face against the stained baize of the desk. She remembered the photograph of the tennis-court at Guise--she remembered the handsome girl at whom Guy Dawnish looked up, laughing. A gust of tears shook her, loosening the dry surface of conventional feeling, welling up from unsuspected depths. She was sorry--very sorry, yet so glad--so ineffably, impenitently glad.

V

There came a reaction in which she decided to write to him. She even sketched out a letter of sisterly, almost motherly, remonstrance, in which she reminded him that he "still had all his life before him." But she reflected that so, after all, had she; and that seemed to weaken the argument.

In the end she decided not to send the letter. He had never spoken to her of his engagement to Gwendolen Matcher, and his letters had contained no allusion to any sentimental disturbance in his life. She had only his few broken words, that night by the river, on which to build her theory of the case. But illuminated by the phrase "an unfortunate attachment" the theory towered up, distinct and immovable, like some high landmark by which travellers shape their course. She had been loved--extraordinarily loved. But he had chosen that she should know of it by his silence rather than by his speech. He had understood that only on those terms could their transcendant communion continue--that he must lose her to keep her. To break that silence would be like spilling a cup of water in a waste of sand. There would be nothing left for her thirst.

Her life, thenceforward, was bathed in a tranquil beauty. The days flowed by like a river beneath the moon--each ripple caught the brightness and passed it on. She began to take a renewed interest in her familiar round of duties. The tasks which had once seemed colourless and irksome had now a kind of sacrificial sweetness, a symbolic meaning into which she alone was initiated. She had been restless--had longed to travel; now she felt that she should never again care to leave Wentworth. But if her desire to wander had ceased, she travelled in spirit, performing invisible pilgrimages in the footsteps of her friend. She regretted that her one short visit to England had taken her so little out of London--that her acquaintance with the landscape had been formed chiefly through the windows of a railway carriage. She threw herself into the architectural studies of the Higher Thought Club, and distinguished herself, at the spring meetings, by her fluency, her competence, her inexhaustible curiosity on the subject of the growth of English Gothic. She ransacked the shelves of the college library, she borrowed photographs of the cathedrals, she pored over the folio pages of "The Seats of Noblemen and Gentlemen." She was like some banished princess who learns that she has inherited a domain in her own country, who knows that she will never see it, yet feels, wherever she walks, its soil beneath her feet.

May was half over, and the Higher Thought Club was to hold its last meeting, previous to the college festivities which, in early June, agreeably disorganized the social routine of Wentworth. The meeting was to take place in Margaret Ransom's drawing-room, and on the day before she sat upstairs preparing for her dual duties as hostess and orator--for she had been invited to read the final paper of the course. In order to sum up with precision her conclusions on the subject of English Gothic she had been rereading an analysis of the structural features of the principal English cathedrals; and she was murmuring over to herself the phrase: "The longitudinal arches of Lincoln have an approximately elliptical form," when there came a knock on the door, and Maria's voice announced: "There's a lady down in the parlour."

Margaret's soul dropped from the heights of the shadowy vaulting to the dead level of an afternoon call at Wentworth.

"A lady? Did she give no name?"

Maria became confused. "She only said she was a lady--" and in reply to her mistress's look of mild surprise: "Well, ma'am, she told me so three or four times over."

Margaret laid her book down, leaving it open at the description of Lincoln, and slowly descended the stairs. As she did so, she repeated to herself: "The longitudinal arches are elliptical."

On the threshold below, she had the odd impression that her bare and inanimate drawing-room was brimming with life and noise--an impression produced, as she presently perceived, by the resolute forward dash--it was almost a pounce--of the one small figure restlessly measuring its length.

The dash checked itself within a yard of Margaret, and the lady--a stranger--held back long enough to stamp on her hostess a sharp impression of sallowness, leanness, keenness, before she said, in a voice that might have been addressing an unruly committee meeting: "I am Lady Caroline Duckett--a fact I found it impossible to make clear to the young woman who let me in."

A warm wave rushed up from Margaret's heart to her throat and forehead. She held out both hands impulsively. "Oh, I'm so glad--I'd no idea--"

Her voice sank under her visitor's impartial scrutiny.

"I don't wonder," said the latter drily. "I suppose she didn't mention, either, that my object in calling here was to see Mrs. Ransom?"

"Oh, yes--won't you sit down?" Margaret pushed a chair forward. She seated herself at a little distance, brain and heart humming with a confused interchange of signals. This dark sharp woman was his aunt--the "clever aunt" who had had such a hard life, but had always managed to keep her head above water. Margaret remembered that Guy had spoken of her kindness--perhaps she would seem kinder when they had talked together a little. Meanwhile the first impression she produced was of an amplitude out of all proportion to her somewhat scant exterior. With her small flat figure, her shabby heterogeneous dress, she was as dowdy as any Professor's wife at Wentworth; but her dowdiness (Margaret borrowed a literary analogy to define it), her dowdiness was somehow "of the centre." Like the insignificant emissary of a great power, she was to be judged rather by her passports than her person.

While Margaret was receiving these impressions, Lady Caroline, with quick bird-like twists of her head, was gathering others from the pale void spaces of the drawing-room. Her eyes, divided by a sharp nose like a bill, seemed to be set far enough apart to see at separate angles; but suddenly she bent both of them on Margaret.

"This _is_ Mrs. Ransom's house?" she asked, with an emphasis on the verb that gave a distinct hint of unfulfilled expectations.

Margaret assented.

"Because your American houses, especially in the provincial towns, all look so remarkably alike, that I thought I might have been mistaken; and as my time is extremely limited--in fact I'm sailing on Wednesday--"

She paused long enough to let Margaret say: "I had no idea you were in this country."

Lady Caroline made no attempt to take this up. "And so much of it," she carried on her sentence, "has been wasted in talking to people I really hadn't the slightest desire to see, that you must excuse me if I go straight to the point."

Margaret felt a sudden tension of the heart. "Of course," she said while a voice within her cried: "He is dead--he has left me a message."

There was another pause; then Lady Caroline went on, with increasing asperity: "So that--in short--if I _could_ see Mrs. Ransom at once--"

Margaret looked up in surprise. "I am Mrs. Ransom," she said.

The other stared a moment, with much the same look of cautious incredulity that had marked her inspection of the drawing-room. Then light came to her.

"Oh, I beg your pardon. I should have said that I wished to see Mrs. _Robert_ Ransom, not Mrs. Ransom. But I understood that in the States you don't make those distinctions." She paused a moment, and then went on, before Margaret could answer: "Perhaps, after all, it's as well that I should see you instead, since you're evidently one of the household--your son and his wife live with you, I suppose? Yes, on the whole, then, it's better--I shall be able to talk so much more frankly." She spoke as if, as a rule, circumstances prevented her giving rein to this propensity. "And frankness, of course, is the only way out of this--this extremely tiresome complication. You know, I suppose, that my nephew thinks he's in love with your daughter-in-law?"

Margaret made a slight movement, but her visitor pressed on without heeding it. "Oh, don't fancy, please, that I'm pretending to take a high moral ground--though his mother does, poor dear! I can perfectly imagine that in a place like this--I've just been driving about it for two hours--a young man of Guy's age would _have_ to provide himself with some sort of distraction, and he's not the kind to go in for anything objectionable. Oh, we quite allow for that--we should allow for the whole affair, if it hadn't so preposterously ended in his throwing over the girl he was engaged to, and upsetting an arrangement that affected a number of people besides himself. I understand that in the States it's different--the young people have only themselves to consider. In England--in our class, I mean--a great deal may depend on a young man's making a good match; and in Guy's case I may say that his mother and sisters (I won't include myself, though I might) have been simply stranded--thrown overboard--by his freak. You can understand how serious it is when I tell you that it's that and nothing else that has brought me all the way to America. And my first idea was to go straight to your daughter-in-law, since her influence is the only thing we can count on now, and put it to her fairly, as I'm putting it to you. But, on the whole, I dare say it's better to see you first--you might give me an idea of the line to take with her. I'm prepared to throw myself on her mercy!"

Margaret rose from her chair, outwardly rigid in proportion to her inward tremor.

"You don't understand--" she began.

Lady Caroline brushed the interruption aside. "Oh, but I do--completely! I cast no reflection on your daughter-in-law.

Guy has made it quite clear to us that his attachment is--has, in short, not been rewarded. But don't you see that that's the worst part of it? There'd be much more hope of his recovering if Mrs. Robert Ransom had--had--"

Margaret's voice broke from her in a cry. "I am Mrs. Robert Ransom," she said.

If Lady Caroline Duckett had hitherto given her hostess the impression of a person not easily silenced, this fact added sensibly to the effect produced by the intense stillness which now fell on her.

She sat quite motionless, her large bangled hands clasped about the meagre fur boa she had unwound from her neck on entering, her rusty black veil pushed up to the edge of a "fringe" of doubtful authenticity, her thin lips parted on a gasp that seemed to sharpen itself on the edges of her teeth. So overwhelming and helpless was her silence that Margaret began to feel a motion of pity beneath her indignation--a desire at least to facilitate the excuses which must terminate their disastrous colloquy. But when Lady Caroline found voice she did not use it to excuse herself.

"You _can't_ be," she said, quite simply.

"Can't be?" Margaret stammered, with a flushing cheek.

"I mean, it's some mistake. Are there _two_ Mrs. Robert Ransoms in the same town? Your family arrangements are so extremely puzzling." She had a farther rush of enlightenment. "Oh, I _see!_ I ought of course to have asked for Mrs. Robert Ransom 'Junior'!"

The idea sent her to her feet with a haste which showed her impatience to make up for lost time.

"There is no other Mrs. Robert Ransom at Wentworth," said Margaret.

"No other--no 'Junior'? Are you _sure?_" Lady Caroline fell back into her seat again. "Then I simply don't see," she murmured helplessly.

Margaret's blush had fixed itself on her throbbing forehead. She remained standing, while her strange visitor continued to gaze at her with a perturbation in which the consciousness of indiscretion had evidently as yet no part.

"I simply don't see," she repeated.

Suddenly she sprang up, and advancing to Margaret laid an inspired hand on her arm. "But, my dear woman, you can help us out all the same; you can help us to find out _who it is_--and you will, won't you? Because, as it's not you, you can't in the least mind what I've been saying--"

Margaret, freeing her arm from her visitor's hold, drew back a step; but Lady Caroline instantly rejoined her.

"Of course, I can see that if it _had_ been, you might have been annoyed: I dare say I put the case stupidly--but I'm so bewildered by this new development--by his using you all this time as a pretext--that I really don't know where to turn for light on the mystery--"

She had Margaret in her imperious grasp again, but the latter broke from her with a more resolute gesture.

"I'm afraid I have no light to give you," she began; but once more Lady Caroline caught her up.

"Oh, but do please understand me! I condemn Guy most strongly for using your name--when we all know you'd been so amazingly kind to him! I haven't a word to say in his defence--but of course the important thing now is: _who is the woman, since you're not?_"

The question rang out loudly, as if all the pale puritan corners of the room flung it back with a shudder at the speaker. In the silence that ensued Margaret felt the blood ebbing back to her heart; then she said, in a distinct and level voice: "I know nothing of the history of Mr. Dawnish."

Lady Caroline gave a stare and a gasp. Her distracted hand groped for her boa and she began to wind it mechanically about her long neck.

"It would really be an enormous help to us--and to poor Gwendolen Matcher," she persisted pleadingly. "And you'd be doing Guy himself a good turn."

Margaret remained silent and motionless while her visitor drew on one of the worn gloves she had pulled off to adjust her veil. Lady Caroline gave the veil a final twitch.

"I've come a tremendously long way," she said, "and, since it isn't you, I can't think why you won't help me. . . ."

When the door had closed on her visitor Margaret Ransom went slowly up the stairs to her room. As she dragged her feet from one step to another, she remembered how she had sprung up the same steep flight after that visit of Guy Dawnish's when she had looked in the glass and seen on her face the blush of youth.

When she reached her room she bolted the door as she had done that day, and again looked at herself in the narrow mirror above her dressing-table. It was just a year since then--the elms were budding again, the willows hanging their green veil above the bench by the river. But there was no trace of youth left in her face--she saw it now as others had doubtless always seen it. If it seemed as it did to Lady Caroline Duckett, what look must it have worn to the fresh gaze of young Guy Dawnish?

A pretext--she had been a pretext. He had used her name to screen some one else--or perhaps merely to escape from a situation of which he was weary. She did not care to conjecture what his motive had been--everything connected with him had grown so remote and alien. She felt no anger--only an unspeakable sadness, a sadness which she knew would never be appeased.

She looked at herself long and steadily; she wished to clear her eyes of all illusions. Then she turned away and took her usual seat beside her work-table. From where she sat she could look down the empty elm-shaded street, up which, at this hour every day, she was sure to see her husband's figure advancing. She would see it presently--she would see it for many years to come. She had a sudden aching sense of the length of the years that stretched before her. Strange that one who was not young should still, in all likelihood, have so long to live!

Nothing was changed in the setting of her life, perhaps nothing would ever change in it. She would certainly live and die in Wentworth. And meanwhile the days would go on as usual, bringing the usual obligations. As the word flitted through her brain she remembered that she had still to put the finishing touches to the paper she was to read the next afternoon at the meeting of the Higher Thought Club.

The book she had been reading lay face downward beside her, where she had left it an hour ago. She took it up, and slowly and painfully, like a child laboriously spelling out the syllables, she went on with the rest of the sentence:

--"and they spring from a level not much above that of the springing of the transverse and diagonal ribs, which are so arranged as to give a convex curve to the surface of the vaulting conoid."

Afterward

I

"OH, THERE IS ONE, OF COURSE, BUT you'll never know it."

The assertion, laughingly flung out six months earlier in a bright June garden, came back to Mary Boyne with a sharp perception of its latent significance as she stood, in the December dusk, waiting for the lamps to be brought into the library.

The words had been spoken by their friend Alida Stair, as they sat at tea on her lawn at Pangbourne, in reference to the very house of which the library in question was the central, the pivotal "feature." Mary Boyne and her husband, in quest of a country place in one of the southern or southwestern counties, had, on their arrival in England, carried their problem straight to Alida Stair, who had successfully solved it in her own case; but it was not until they had rejected, almost capriciously, several practical and judicious suggestions that she threw it out: "Well, there's Lyng, in Dorsetshire. It belongs to Hugo's cousins, and you can get it for a song."

The reasons she gave for its being obtainable on these terms -- its remoteness from a station, its lack of electric light, hot-water pipes, and other vulgar necessities -- were exactly those pleading in its favor with two romantic Americans perversely in search of the economic drawbacks which were associated, in their tradition, with unusual architectural felicities.

"I should never believe I was living in an old house unless I was thoroughly uncomfortable," Ned Boyne, the more extravagant of the two, had jocosely insisted; "the least hint of 'convenience' would make me think it had been bought out of an exhibition, with the pieces numbered, and set up again." And they had proceeded to enumerate, with humorous precision, their various suspicions and exactions, refusing to believe that the house their cousin recommended was really Tudor till they learned it had no heating system, or that the village church was literally in the grounds till she assured them of the deplorable uncertainty of the watersupply.

"It's too uncomfortable to be true!" Edward Boyne had continued to exult as the avowal of each disadvantage was successively wrung from her; but he had cut short his rhapsody to ask, with a sudden relapse to distrust: "And the ghost? You've been concealing from us the fact that there is no ghost!"

Mary, at the moment, had laughed with him, yet almost with her laugh, being possessed of several sets of independent perceptions, had noted a sudden flatness of tone in Alida's answering hilarity.

"Oh, Dorsetshire's full of ghosts, you know."

"Yes, yes; but that won't do. I don't want to have to drive ten miles to see somebody else's ghost. I want one of my own on the premises. Is there a ghost at Lyng?"

His rejoinder had made Alida laugh again, and it was then that she had flung back tantalizingly: "Oh, there is one, of course, but you'll never know it."

"Never know it?" Boyne pulled her up. "But what in the world constitutes a ghost except the fact of its being known for one?"

"I can't say. But that's the story."

"That there's a ghost, but that nobody knows it's a ghost?"

"Well -- not till afterward, at any rate."

"Till afterward?"

"Not till long, long afterward."

"But if it's once been identified as an unearthly visitant, why hasn't its signalement been handed down in the family? How has it managed to preserve its incognito?"

Alida could only shake her head. "Don't ask me. But it has."

"And then suddenly --" Mary spoke up as if from some cavernous depth of divination --"suddenly, long afterward, one says to one's self, 'That was it?'"

She was oddly startled at the sepulchral sound with which her question fell on the banter of the other two, and she saw the shadow of the same surprise flit across Alida's clear pupils. "I suppose so. One just has to wait."

"Oh, hang waiting!" Ned broke in. "Life's too short for a ghost who can only be enjoyed in retrospect. Can't we do better than that, Mary?"

But it turned out that in the event they were not destined to, for within three months of their conversation with Mrs. Stair they were established at Lyng, and the life they had yearned for to the point of planning it out in all its daily details had actually begun for them.

It was to sit, in the thick December dusk, by just such a widehooded fireplace, under just such black oak rafters, with the sense that beyond the mullioned panes the downs were darkening to a deeper solitude: it was for the ultimate indulgence in such sensations that Mary Boyne had endured for nearly fourteen years the soul-deadening ugliness of the Middle West, and that Boyne had ground on doggedly at his engineering till, with a suddenness that still made her blink, the prodigious windfall of the Blue Star Mine had put them at a stroke in possession of life and the leisure to taste it. They had never for a moment meant their new state to be one of idleness; but they meant to give themselves only to harmonious activities. She had her vision of painting and gardening (against a background of gray walls), he dreamed of the production of his long-planned book on the "Economic Basis of Culture"; and with such absorbing work ahead no existence could be too sequestered; they could not get far enough from the world, or plunge deep enough into the past.

Dorsetshire had attracted them from the first by a semblance of remoteness out of all proportion to its geographical position. But to the Boynes it was one of the ever-recurring wonders of the whole incredibly compressed island -- a nest of counties, as they put it -- that for the production of its effects so little of a given quality went so far: that so few miles made a distance, and so short a distance a difference.

"It's that," Ned had once enthusiastically explained, "that gives such depth to their effects, such relief to their least contrasts. They've been able to lay the butter so thick on every exquisite mouthful."

The butter had certainly been laid on thick at Lyng: the old gray house, hidden under a shoulder of the downs, had almost all the finer marks of commerce with a protracted past. The mere fact that it was neither large nor exceptional made it, to the Boynes, abound the more richly in its special sense -- the sense of having been for centuries a deep, dim reservoir of life. The life had probably not been of the most vivid order: for long periods, no doubt, it had fallen as noiselessly into the past as the quiet drizzle of autumn fell, hour after hour, into the green fish-pond between the yews; but these back-waters of existence sometimes breed, in their sluggish depths, strange acuities of emotion, and Mary Boyne had felt from the first the occasional brush of an intenser memory.

The feeling had never been stronger than on the December afternoon when, waiting in the library for the belated lamps, she rose from her seat and stood among the shadows of the hearth. Her husband had gone off, after luncheon, for one of his long tramps on the downs. She had noticed of late that he preferred to be unaccompanied on these occasions; and, in the tried security of their personal relations, had been driven to conclude that his book was bothering him, and that he needed the afternoons to turn over in solitude the problems left from the morning's work. Certainly the book was not going as smoothly as she had imagined it would, and the lines of perplexity between his eyes had never been there in his engineering days. Then he had often looked fagged to the verge of illness, but the native demon of "worry" had never branded his brow. Yet the few pages he had so far read to her -- the introduction, and a synopsis of the opening chapter -- gave evidences of a firm possession of his subject, and a deepening confidence in his powers.

The fact threw her into deeper perplexity, since, now that he had done with "business" and its disturbing contingencies, the one other possible element of anxiety was eliminated. Unless it were his health, then? But physically he had gained since they had come to Dorsetshire, grown robuster, ruddier, and fresher-eyed. It was only within a week that she had felt in him the undefinable change that made her restless in his absence, and as tongue-tied in his presence as though it were she who had a secret to keep from him!

The thought that there was a secret somewhere between them struck her with a sudden smart rap of wonder, and she looked about her down the dim, long room.

"Can it be the house?" she mused.

The room itself might have been full of secrets. They seemed to be piling themselves up, as evening fell, like the layers and layers of velvet shadow dropping from the low ceiling, the dusky walls of books, the smoke-blurred sculpture of the hooded hearth.

"Why, of course -- the house is haunted!" she reflected.

The ghost -- Alida's imperceptible ghost -- after figuring largely in the banter of their first month or two at Lyng, had been gradually discarded as too ineffectual for imaginative use. Mary had, indeed, as became the tenant of a haunted house, made the customary inquiries among her few rural neighbors, but, beyond a vague, "They du say so, Ma'am," the villagers had nothing to impart. The elusive specter had apparently never had sufficient identity for a legend to crystallize about it, and after a time the Boynes had laughingly set the matter down to their profitand-loss account, agreeing that Lyng was one of the few houses good enough in itself to dispense with supernatural enhancements.

"And I suppose, poor, ineffectual demon, that's why it beats its beautiful wings in vain in the void," Mary had laughingly concluded.

"Or, rather," Ned answered, in the same strain, "why, amid so much that's ghostly, it can never affirm its separate existence as the ghost." And thereupon their invisible housemate had finally dropped out of their references, which were numerous enough to make them promptly unaware of the loss.

Now, as she stood on the hearth, the subject of their earlier curiosity revived in her with a new sense of its meaning -- a sense gradually acquired through close daily contact with the scene of the lurking mystery. It was the house itself, of course, that possessed the ghost-seeing faculty, that communed visually but secretly with its own past; and if one could only get into close enough communion with the house, one might surprise its secret, and acquire the ghost-sight on one's own account. Perhaps, in his long solitary hours in this very room, where she never trespassed till the afternoon, her husband had acquired it already, and was silently carrying the dread weight of whatever it had revealed to him. Mary was too well-versed in the code of the spectral world not to know that one could not talk about the ghosts one saw: to do so was almost as great a breach of goodbreeding as to name a lady in a club. But this explanation did not really satisfy her. "What, after all, except for the fun of the frisson," she reflected, "would he really care for any of their old ghosts?" And thence she was thrown back once more on the fundamental dilemma: the fact that one's greater or less susceptibility to spectral influences had no particular bearing on the case, since, when one did see a ghost at Lyng, one did not know it.

"Not till long afterward," Alida Stair had said. Well, supposing Ned had seen one when they first came, and had known only within the last week what had happened to him? More and more under the spell of the hour, she threw back her searching thoughts to the early days of their tenancy, but at first only to recall a gay confusion of unpacking, settling, arranging of books, and calling to each other from remote corners of the house as treasure after treasure of their habitation revealed itself to them. It was in this particular connection that she presently recalled a certain soft afternoon of the previous October, when, passing from the first rapturous flurry of exploration to a detailed inspection of the old house, she had pressed (like a novel heroine) a panel that opened at her touch, on a narrow flight of stairs leading to an unsuspected flat ledge of the roof -- the roof which, from below, seemed to slope away on all sides too abruptly for any but practised feet to scale.

The view from this hidden coign was enchanting, and she had flown down to snatch Ned from his papers and give him the freedom of her discovery. She remembered still how, standing on the narrow ledge, he had passed his arm about her while their gaze flew to the long, tossed horizon-line of the downs, and then dropped contentedly back to trace the arabesque of yew hedges about the fish-pond, and the shadow of the cedar on the lawn.

"And now the other way," he had said, gently turning her about within his arm; and closely pressed to him, she had absorbed, like some long, satisfying draft, the picture of the gray walled court, the squat lions on the gates, and the lime-avenue reaching up to the highroad under the downs.

It was just then, while they gazed and held each other, that she had felt his arm relax, and heard a sharp "Hullo!" that made her turn to glance at him.

Distinctly, yes, she now recalled she had seen, as she glanced, a shadow of anxiety, of perplexity, rather, fall across his face; and, following his eyes, had beheld the figure of a man -- a man in loose, grayish clothes, as it appeared to her -- who was sauntering down the lime-avenue to the court with the tentative gait of a stranger seeking his way. Her short-sighted eyes had given her but a blurred impression of slightness and grayness, with something foreign, or at least unlocal, in the cut of the figure or its garb; but her husband had apparently seen more -- seen enough to make him push past her with a sharp "Wait!" and dash down the twisting stairs without pausing to give her a hand for the descent.

A slight tendency to dizziness obliged her, after a provisional clutch at the chimney against which they had been leaning, to follow him down more cautiously; and when she had reached the attic landing she paused again for a less definite reason, leaning over the oak banister to strain her eyes through the silence of the brown, sun-flecked depths below. She lingered there till, somewhere in those depths, she heard the closing of a door; then, mechanically impelled, she went down the shallow flights of steps till she reached the lower hall.

The front door stood open on the mild sunlight of the court, and hall and court were empty. The library door was open, too, and after listening in vain for any sound of voices within, she quickly crossed the threshold, and found her husband alone, vaguely fingering the papers on his desk.

He looked up, as if surprised at her precipitate entrance, but the shadow of anxiety had passed from his face, leaving it even, as she fancied, a little brighter and clearer than usual.

"What was it? Who was it?" she asked.

"Who?" he repeated, with the surprise still all on his side.

"The man we saw coming toward the house."

He seemed honestly to reflect. "The man? Why, I thought I saw Peters; I dashed after him to say a word about the stable-drains, but he had disappeared before I could get down."

"Disappeared? Why, he seemed to be walking so slowly when we saw him."

Boyne shrugged his shoulders. "So I thought; but he must

have got up steam in the interval. What do you say to our trying a scramble up Meldon Steep before sunset?"

That was all. At the time the occurrence had been less than nothing, had, indeed, been immediately obliterated by the magic of their first vision from Meldon Steep, a height which they had dreamed of climbing ever since they had first seen its bare spine heaving itself above the low roof of Lyng. Doubtless it was the mere fact of the other incident's having occurred on the very day of their ascent to Meldon that had kept it stored away in the unconscious fold of association from which it now emerged; for in itself it had no mark of the portentous. At the moment there could have been nothing more natural than that Ned should dash himself from the roof in the pursuit of dilatory tradesmen. It was the period when they were always on the watch for one or the other of the specialists employed about the place; always lying in wait for them, and dashing out at them with questions, reproaches, or reminders. And certainly in the distance the gray figure had looked like Peters.

Yet now, as she reviewed the rapid scene, she felt her husband's explanation of it to have been invalidated by the look of anxiety on his face. Why had the familiar appearance of Peters made him anxious? Why, above all, if it was of such prime necessity to confer with that authority on the subject of the stable-drains, had the failure to find him produced such a look of relief? Mary could not say that any one of these considerations had occurred to her at the time, yet, from the promptness with which they now marshaled themselves at her summons, she had a sudden sense that they must all along have been there, waiting their hour.

II

Weary with her thoughts, she moved toward the window. The library was now completely dark, and she was surprised to see how much faint light the outer world still held.

As she peered out into it across the court, a figure shaped itself in the tapering perspective of bare lines: it looked a mere blot of deeper gray in the grayness, and for an instant, as it moved toward her, her heart thumped to the thought, "It's the ghost!"

She had time, in that long instant, to feel suddenly that the man of whom, two months earlier, she had a brief distant vision from the roof was now, at his predestined hour, about to reveal himself as not having been Peters; and her spirit sank under the impending fear of the disclosure. But almost with the next tick of the clock the ambiguous figure, gaining substance and character, showed itself even to her weak sight as her husband's; and she turned away to meet him, as he entered, with the confession of her folly.

"It's really too absurd," she laughed out from the threshold, "but I never can remember!"

"Remember what?" Boyne questioned as they drew together.

"That when one sees the Lyng ghost one never knows it."

Her hand was on his sleeve, and he kept it there, but with no response in his gesture or in the lines of his fagged, preoccupied face.

"Did you think you'd seen it?" he asked, after an appreciable interval.

"Why, I actually took you for it, my dear, in my mad determination to spot it!"

"Me -- just now?" His arm dropped away, and he turned from her with a faint echo of her laugh. "Really, dearest, you'd better give it up, if that's the best you can do."

"Yes, I give it up -- I give it up. Have you?" she asked, turning round on him abruptly.

The parlor-maid had entered with letters and a lamp, and the light struck up into Boyne's face as he bent above the tray she presented.

"Have you?" Mary perversely insisted, when the servant had disappeared on her errand of illumination.

"Have I what?" he rejoined absently, the light bringing out the sharp stamp of worry between his brows as he turned over the letters.

"Given up trying to see the ghost." Her heart beat a little at the experiment she was making.

Her husband, laying his letters aside, moved away into the shadow of the hearth.

"I never tried," he said, tearing open the wrapper of a newspaper.

"Well, of course," Mary persisted, "the exasperating thing is that there's no use trying, since one can't be sure till so long afterward."

He was unfolding the paper as if he had hardly heard her; but after a pause, during which the sheets rustled spasmodically between his hands, he lifted his head to say abruptly, "Have you any idea how long?"

Mary had sunk into a low chair beside the fireplace. From her seat she looked up, startled, at her husband's profile, which was darkly projected against the circle of lamplight.

"No; none. Have YOU?" she retorted, repeating her former phrase with an added keenness of intention.

Boyne crumpled the paper into a bunch, and then inconsequently turned back with it toward the lamp.

"Lord, no! I only meant," he explained, with a faint tinge of impatience, "is there any legend, any tradition, as to that?"

"Not that I know of," she answered; but the impulse to add, "What makes you ask?" was checked by the reappearance of the parlormaid with tea and a second lamp.

With the dispersal of shadows, and the repetition of the daily domestic office, Mary Boyne felt herself less oppressed by that sense of something mutely imminent which had darkened her solitary afternoon. For a few moments she gave herself silently to the details of her task, and when she looked up from it she was struck to the point of bewilderment by the change in her husband's face. He had seated himself near the farther lamp, and was absorbed in the perusal of his letters; but was it something he had found in them, or merely the shifting of her own point of view, that had restored his features to their normal aspect? The longer she looked, the more definitely the change affirmed itself. The lines of painful tension had vanished, and such traces of fatigue as lingered were of the kind easily attributable to steady mental effort. He glanced up, as if drawn by her gaze, and met her eyes with a smile.

"I'm dying for my tea, you know; and here's a letter for you," he said.

She took the letter he held out in exchange for the cup she proffered him, and, returning to her seat, broke the seal with the languid gesture of the reader whose interests are all inclosed in the circle of one cherished presence.

Her next conscious motion was that of starting to her feet, the letter falling to them as she rose, while she held out to her husband a long newspaper clipping.

"Ned! What's this? What does it mean?"

He had risen at the same instant, almost as if hearing her cry before she uttered it; and for a perceptible space of time he and she studied each other, like adversaries watching for an advantage, across the space between her chair and his desk.

"What's what? You fairly made me jump!" Boyne said at length, moving toward her with a sudden, half-exasperated laugh. The shadow of apprehension was on his face again, not now a look of fixed foreboding, but a shifting vigilance of lips and eyes that gave her the sense of his feeling himself invisibly surrounded.

Her hand shook so that she could hardly give him the clipping.

"This article -- from the 'Waukesha Sentinel' -- that a man named Elwell has brought suit against you -- that there was something wrong about the Blue Star Mine. I can't understand more than half."

They continued to face each other as she spoke, and to her astonishment, she saw that her words had the almost immediate effect of dissipating the strained watchfulness of his look.

"Oh, that!" He glanced down the printed slip, and then folded it with the gesture of one who handles something harmless and familiar. "What's the matter with you this afternoon, Mary? I thought you'd got bad news."

She stood before him with her undefinable terror subsiding slowly under the reassuring touch of his composure.

"You knew about this, then -- it's all right?"

"Certainly I knew about it; and it's all right."

"But what is it? I don't understand. What does this man accuse you of?"

"Oh, pretty nearly every crime in the calendar." Boyne had

tossed the clipping down, and thrown himself comfortably into an arm-chair near the fire. "Do you want to hear the story? It's not particularly interesting -- just a squabble over interests in the Blue Star."

"But who is this Elwell? I don't know the name."

"Oh, he's a fellow I put into it -- gave him a hand up. I told you all about him at the time."

"I daresay. I must have forgotten." Vainly she strained back among her memories. "But if you helped him, why does he make this return?"

"Oh, probably some shyster lawyer got hold of him and talked him over. It's all rather technical and complicated. I thought that kind of thing bored you."

His wife felt a sting of compunction. Theoretically, she deprecated the American wife's detachment from her husband's professional interests, but in practice she had always found it difficult to fix her attention on Boyne's report of the transactions in which his varied interests involved him. Besides, she had felt from the first that, in a community where the amenities of living could be obtained only at the cost of efforts as arduous as her husband's professional labors, such brief leisure as they could command should be used as an escape from immediate preoccupations, a flight to the life they always dreamed of living. Once or twice, now that this new life had actually drawn its magic circle about them, she had asked herself if she had done right; but hitherto such conjectures had been no more than the retrospective excursions of an active fancy. Now, for the first time, it startled her a little to find how little she knew of the material foundation on which her happiness was built.

She glanced again at her husband, and was reassured by the composure of his face; yet she felt the need of more definite grounds for her reassurance.

"But doesn't this suit worry you? Why have you never spoken to me about it?"

He answered both questions at once: "I didn't speak of it at first because it did worry me -- annoyed me, rather. But it's all ancient history now. Your correspondent must have got hold of a back number of the 'Sentinel.'"

She felt a quick thrill of relief. "You mean it's over? He's lost his case?"

There was a just perceptible delay in Boyne's reply. "The suit's been withdrawn -- that's all."

But she persisted, as if to exonerate herself from the inward charge of being too easily put off. "Withdrawn because he saw he had no chance?"

"Oh, he had no chance," Boyne answered.

She was still struggling with a dimly felt perplexity at the back of her thoughts.

"How long ago was it withdrawn?"

He paused, as if with a slight return of his former

uncertainty. "I've just had the news now; but I've been expecting it."

"Just now -- in one of your letters?"

"Yes; in one of my letters."

She made no answer, and was aware only, after a short interval of waiting, that he had risen, and strolling across the room, had placed himself on the sofa at her side. She felt him, as he did so, pass an arm about her, she felt his hand seek hers and clasp it, and turning slowly, drawn by the warmth of his cheek, she met the smiling clearness of his eyes.

"It's all right -- it's all right?" she questioned, through the flood of her dissolving doubts; and "I give you my word it never was righter!" he laughed back at her, holding her close.

III

One of the strangest things she was afterward to recall out of all the next day's incredible strangeness was the sudden and complete recovery of her sense of security.

It was in the air when she woke in her low-ceilinged, dusky room; it accompanied her down-stairs to the breakfast-table, flashed out at her from the fire, and re-duplicated itself brightly from the flanks of the urn and the sturdy flutings of the Georgian teapot. It was as if, in some roundabout way, all her diffused apprehensions of the previous day, with their moment of sharp concentration about the newspaper article,

-- as if this dim questioning of the future, and startled return upon the past,-had between them liquidated the arrears of some haunting moral obligation. If she had indeed been careless of her husband's affairs, it was, her new state seemed to prove, because her faith in him instinctively justified such carelessness; and his right to her faith had overwhelmingly affirmed itself in the very face of menace and suspicion. She had never seen him more untroubled, more naturally and unconsciously in possession of himself, than after the cross-examination to which she had subjected him: it was almost as if he had been aware of her lurking doubts, and had wanted the air cleared as much as she did.

It was as clear, thank Heaven! as the bright outer light that surprised her almost with a touch of summer when she issued from the house for her daily round of the gardens. She had left Boyne at his desk, indulging herself, as she passed the library door, by a last peep at his quiet face, where he bent, pipe in his mouth, above his papers, and now she had her own morning's task to perform. The task involved on such charmed winter days almost as much delighted loitering about the different quarters of her demesne as if spring were already at work on shrubs and borders. There were such inexhaustible possibilities still before her, such opportunities to bring out the latent graces of the old place, without a single irreverent touch of alteration, that the winter months were all too short to plan what spring and autumn executed. And her recovered sense of safety gave, on this particular morning, a peculiar zest to her progress through the sweet, still place. She went first to the kitchen-garden, where the espaliered pear-trees drew complicated patterns on the walls, and pigeons were fluttering and preening about the silvery-slated roof of their cot. There was something wrong about the piping of the hothouse, and she was expecting an authority from Dorchester, who was to drive out between trains and make a diagnosis of the boiler. But when she dipped into the damp heat of the greenhouses, among the spiced scents and waxy pinks and reds of old-fashioned exotics, -- even the flora of Lyng was in the note!-she learned that the great man had not arrived, and the day being too rare to waste in an artificial atmosphere, she came out again and paced slowly along the springy turf of the bowling-green to the gardens behind the house. At their farther end rose a grass terrace, commanding, over the fish-pond and the yew hedges, a view of the long house-front, with its twisted chimney-stacks and the blue shadows of its roof angles, all drenched in the pale gold moisture of the air.

Seen thus, across the level tracery of the yews, under the suffused, mild light, it sent her, from its open windows and hospitably smoking chimneys, the look of some warm human presence, of a mind slowly ripened on a sunny wall of experience. She had never before had so deep a sense of her intimacy with it, such a conviction that its secrets were all beneficent, kept, as they said to children, "for one's good," so complete a trust in its power to gather up her life and Ned's into the harmonious pattern of the long, long story it sat there weaving in the sun.

She heard steps behind her, and turned, expecting to see the gardener, accompanied by the engineer from Dorchester. But only one figure was in sight, that of a youngish, slightly built man, who, for reasons she could not on the spot have specified, did not remotely resemble her preconceived notion of an authority on hot-house boilers. The new-comer, on seeing her, lifted his hat, and paused with the air of a gentleman -- perhaps a traveler-desirous of having it immediately known that his intrusion is involuntary. The local fame of Lyng occasionally attracted the more intelligent sight-seer, and Mary half-expected to see the stranger dissemble a camera, or justify his presence by producing it. But he made no gesture of any sort, and after a moment she asked, in a tone responding to the courteous deprecation of his attitude: "Is there any one you wish to see?"

"I came to see Mr. Boyne," he replied. His intonation, rather than his accent, was faintly American, and Mary, at the familiar note, looked at him more closely. The brim of his soft felt hat cast a shade on his face, which, thus obscured, wore to her short-sighted gaze a look of seriousness, as of a person arriving "on business," and civilly but firmly aware of his rights.

Past experience had made Mary equally sensible to such claims; but she was jealous of her husband's morning hours, and doubtful of his having given any one the right to intrude on them.

"Have you an appointment with Mr. Boyne?" she asked.

He hesitated, as if unprepared for the question.

"Not exactly an appointment," he replied.

"Then I'm afraid, this being his working-time, that he can't receive you now. Will you give me a message, or come back later?"

The visitor, again lifting his hat, briefly replied that he would come back later, and walked away, as if to regain the front of the house. As his figure receded down the walk between the yew hedges, Mary saw him pause and look up an instant at the peaceful house-front bathed in faint winter sunshine; and it struck her, with a tardy touch of compunction, that it would have been more humane to ask if he had come from a distance, and to offer, in that case, to inquire if her husband could receive him. But as the thought occurred to her he passed out of sight behind a pyramidal yew, and at the same moment her attention was distracted by the approach of the gardener, attended by the bearded pepper-and-salt figure of the boiler-maker from Dorchester.

The encounter with this authority led to such far-reaching issues that they resulted in his finding it expedient to ignore his train, and beguiled Mary into spending the remainder of the morning in absorbed confabulation among the greenhouses. She was startled to find, when the colloquy ended, that it was nearly luncheon-time, and she half expected, as she hurried back to the house, to see her husband coming out to meet her. But she found no one in the court but an under-gardener raking the gravel, and the hall, when she entered it, was so silent that she guessed Boyne to be still at work behind the closed door of the library.

Not wishing to disturb him, she turned into the drawing-room, and there, at her writing-table, lost herself in renewed calculations of the outlay to which the morning's conference had committed her. The knowledge that she could permit herself such follies had not yet lost its novelty; and somehow, in contrast to the vague apprehensions of the previous days, it now seemed an element of her recovered security, of the sense that, as Ned had said, things in general had never been "righter."

She was still luxuriating in a lavish play of figures when the parlor-maid, from the threshold, roused her with a dubiously worded inquiry as to the expediency of serving luncheon. It was one of their jokes that Trimmle announced luncheon as if she were divulging a state secret, and Mary, intent upon her papers, merely murmured an absent-minded assent.

She felt Trimmle wavering expressively on the threshold as if in rebuke of such offhand acquiescence; then her retreating steps sounded down the passage, and Mary, pushing away her papers, crossed the hall, and went to the library door. It was still closed, and she wavered in her turn, disliking to disturb her husband, yet anxious that he should not exceed his normal measure of work. As she stood there, balancing her impulses, the esoteric Trimmle returned with the announcement of luncheon, and Mary, thus impelled, opened the door and went into the library.

Boyne was not at his desk, and she peered about her, expecting to discover him at the book-shelves, somewhere down the length of the room; but her call brought no response, and gradually it became clear to her that he was not in the library.

She turned back to the parlor-maid.

"Mr. Boyne must be up-stairs. Please tell him that luncheon is ready."

The parlor-maid appeared to hesitate between the obvious duty of obeying orders and an equally obvious conviction of the foolishness of the injunction laid upon her. The struggle resulted in her saying doubtfully, "If you please, Madam, Mr. Boyne's not up-stairs."

"Not in his room? Are you sure?"

"I'm sure, Madam."

Mary consulted the clock. "Where is he, then?"

"He's gone out," Trimmle announced, with the superior air of one who has respectfully waited for the question that a well-ordered mind would have first propounded.

Mary's previous conjecture had been right, then. Boyne must have gone to the gardens to meet her, and since she had missed him, it was clear that he had taken the shorter way by the south door, instead of going round to the court. She crossed the hall to the glass portal opening directly on the yew garden, but the parlormaid, after another moment of inner conflict, decided to bring out recklessly, "Please, Madam, Mr. Boyne didn't go that way."

Mary turned back. "Where did he go? And when?"

"He went out of the front door, up the drive, Madam." It was a matter of principle with Trimmle never to answer more than one question at a time.

"Up the drive? At this hour?" Mary went to the door herself, and glanced across the court through the long tunnel of bare limes. But its perspective was as empty as when she had scanned it on entering the house.

"Did Mr. Boyne leave no message?" she asked.

Trimmle seemed to surrender herself to a last struggle with the forces of chaos.

"No, Madam. He just went out with the gentleman."

"The gentleman? What gentleman?" Mary wheeled about, as if to front this new factor.

"The gentleman who called, Madam," said Trimmle, resignedly.

"When did a gentleman call? Do explain yourself, Trimmle!"

Only the fact that Mary was very hungry, and that she wanted to consult her husband about the greenhouses, would have caused her to lay so unusual an injunction on her attendant; and even now she was detached enough to note in Trimmle's eye the dawning defiance of the respectful subordinate who has been pressed too hard.

"I couldn't exactly say the hour, Madam, because I didn't let the gentleman in," she replied, with the air of magnanimously ignoring the irregularity of her mistress's course.

"You didn't let him in?"

"No, Madam. When the bell rang I was dressing, and Agnes --"

"Go and ask Agnes, then," Mary interjected. Trimmle still wore her look of patient magnanimity. "Agnes would not know, Madam, for she had unfortunately burnt her hand in trying the wick of the new lamp from town --" Trimmle, as Mary was aware, had always been opposed to the new lamp --"and so Mrs. Dockett sent the kitchen-maid instead."

Mary looked again at the clock. "It's after two! Go and ask the kitchen-maid if Mr. Boyne left any word."

She went into luncheon without waiting, and Trimmle presently brought her there the kitchen-maid's statement that the gentleman had called about one o'clock, that Mr. Boyne had gone out with him without leaving any message. The kitchen-maid did not even know the caller's name, for he had written it on a slip of paper, which he had folded and handed to her, with the injunction to deliver it at once to Mr. Boyne.

Mary finished her luncheon, still wondering, and when it was over, and Trimmle had brought the coffee to the drawing-room, her wonder had deepened to a first faint tinge of disquietude. It was unlike Boyne to absent himself without explanation at so unwonted an hour, and the difficulty of identifying the visitor whose summons he had apparently obeyed made his disappearance the more unaccountable. Mary Boyne's experience as the wife of a busy engineer, subject to sudden calls and compelled to keep irregular hours, had trained her to the philosophic acceptance of surprises; but since Boyne's withdrawal from business he had adopted a Benedictine regularity of life. As if to make up for the dispersed and agitated years, with their "stand-up" lunches and dinners rattled down to the joltings of the dining-car, he cultivated the last refinements of punctuality and monotony, discouraging his wife's fancy for the unexpected; and declaring that to a delicate taste there were infinite gradations of pleasure in the fixed recurrences of habit.

Still, since no life can completely defend itself from the unforeseen, it was evident that all Boyne's precautions would sooner or later prove unavailable, and Mary concluded that he had cut short a tiresome visit by walking with his caller to the station, or at least accompanying him for part of the way.

This conclusion relieved her from farther preoccupation, and she went out herself to take up her conference with the gardener. Thence she walked to the village post-office, a mile or so away; and when she turned toward home, the early twilight was setting in.

She had taken a foot-path across the downs, and as Boyne, meanwhile, had probably returned from the station by the highroad, there was little likelihood of their meeting on the way. She felt sure, however, of his having reached the house before her; so sure that, when she entered it herself, without even pausing to inquire of Trimmle, she made directly for the library. But the library was still empty, and with an unwonted precision of visual memory she immediately observed that the papers on her husband's desk lay precisely as they had lain when she had gone in to call him to luncheon.

Then of a sudden she was seized by a vague dread of the unknown. She had closed the door behind her on entering, and as she stood alone in the long, silent, shadowy room, her dread seemed to take shape and sound, to be there audibly breathing and lurking among the shadows. Her short-sighted eyes strained through them, halfdiscerning an actual presence, something aloof, that watched and knew; and in the recoil from that intangible propinquity she threw herself suddenly on the bell-rope and gave it a desperate pull.

The long, quavering summons brought Trimmle in precipitately with a lamp, and Mary breathed again at this sobering reappearance of the usual.

"You may bring tea if Mr. Boyne is in," she said, to justify her ring.

"Very well, Madam. But Mr. Boyne is not in," said Trimmle, putting down the lamp.

"Not in? You mean he's come back and gone out again?"

"No, Madam. He's never been back."

The dread stirred again, and Mary knew that now it had her fast.

"Not since he went out with -- the gentleman?"

"Not since he went out with the gentleman."

"But who was the gentleman?" Mary gasped out, with the sharp note of some one trying to be heard through a confusion of meaningless noises.

"That I couldn't say, Madam." Trimmle, standing there by the lamp, seemed suddenly to grow less round and rosy, as though eclipsed by the same creeping shade of apprehension.

"But the kitchen-maid knows -- wasn't it the kitchen-maid who let him in?"

"She doesn't know either, Madam, for he wrote his name on a folded paper."

Mary, through her agitation, was aware that they were both designating the unknown visitor by a vague pronoun, instead of the conventional formula which, till then, had kept their allusions within the bounds of custom. And at the same moment her mind caught at the suggestion of the folded paper.

"But he must have a name! Where is the paper?"

She moved to the desk, and began to turn over the scattered documents that littered it. The first that caught her eye was an unfinished letter in her husband's hand, with his pen lying across it, as though dropped there at a sudden summons.

"My dear Parvis," -- who was Parvis? --"I have just received your letter announcing Elwell's death, and while I suppose there is now no farther risk of trouble, it might be safer --"

She tossed the sheet aside, and continued her search; but no folded paper was discoverable among the letters and pages of manuscript which had been swept together in a promiscuous heap, as if by a hurried or a startled gesture.

"But the kitchen-maid saw him. Send her here," she commanded, wondering at her dullness in not thinking sooner of so simple a solution.

Trimmle, at the behest, vanished in a flash, as if thankful to be out of the room, and when she reappeared, conducting the agitated underling, Mary had regained her self-possession, and had her questions pat.

The gentleman was a stranger, yes -- that she understood. But what had he said? And, above all, what had he looked like? The first question was easily enough answered, for the disconcerting reason that he had said so little -- had merely asked for Mr. Boyne, and, scribbling something on a bit of paper, had requested that it should at once be carried in to him.

"Then you don't know what he wrote? You're not sure it was his name?"

The kitchen-maid was not sure, but supposed it was, since he had written it in answer to her inquiry as to whom she should announce.

"And when you carried the paper in to Mr. Boyne, what did he say?"

The kitchen-maid did not think that Mr. Boyne had said anything, but she could not be sure, for just as she had handed him the paper and he was opening it, she had become aware that the visitor had followed her into the library, and she had slipped out, leaving the two gentlemen together.

"But then, if you left them in the library, how do you know that they went out of the house?"

This question plunged the witness into momentary inarticulateness, from which she was rescued by Trimmle, who, by means of ingenious circumlocutions, elicited the statement that before she could cross the hall to the back passage she had heard the gentlemen behind her, and had seen them go out of the front door together.

"Then, if you saw the gentleman twice, you must be able to tell me what he looked like."

But with this final challenge to her powers of expression it became clear that the limit of the kitchen-maid's endurance had been reached. The obligation of going to the front door to "show in" a visitor was in itself so subversive of the fundamental order of things that it had thrown her faculties into hopeless disarray, and she could only stammer out, after various panting efforts at evocation, "His hat, mum, was different-like, as you might say --"

"Different? How different?" Mary flashed out at her, her own mind, in the same instant, leaping back to an image left on it that morning, but temporarily lost under layers of subsequent impressions.

"His hat had a wide brim, you mean? and his face was pale -- a youngish face?" Mary pressed her, with a white-lipped intensity of interrogation. But if the kitchen-maid found any adequate answer to this challenge, it was swept away for her listener down the rushing current of her own convictions. The stranger -- the stranger in the garden! Why had Mary not thought of him before? She needed no one now to tell her that it was he who had called for her husband and gone away with him. But who was he, and why had Boyne obeyed his call?

IV

It leaped out at her suddenly, like a grin out of the dark, that they had often called England so little --"such a confoundedly hard place to get lost in."

A confoundedly hard place to get lost in! That had been

her husband's phrase. And now, with the whole machinery of official investigation sweeping its flash-lights from shore to shore, and across the dividing straits; now, with Boyne's name blazing from the walls of every town and village, his portrait (how that wrung her!) hawked up and down the country like the image of a hunted criminal; now the little compact, populous island, so policed, surveyed, and administered, revealed itself as a Sphinx-like guardian of abysmal mysteries, staring back into his wife's anguished eyes as if with the malicious joy of knowing something they would never know!

In the fortnight since Boyne's disappearance there had been no word of him, no trace of his movements. Even the usual misleading reports that raise expectancy in tortured bosoms had been few and fleeting. No one but the bewildered kitchen-maid had seen him leave the house, and no one else had seen "the gentleman" who accompanied him. All inquiries in the neighborhood failed to elicit the memory of a stranger's presence that day in the neighborhood of Lyng. And no one had met Edward Boyne, either alone or in company, in any of the neighboring villages, or on the road across the downs, or at either of the local railway-stations. The sunny English noon had swallowed him as completely as if he had gone out into Cimmerian night.

Mary, while every external means of investigation was working at its highest pressure, had ransacked her husband's papers for any trace of antecedent complications, of entanglements or obligations unknown to her, that might throw a faint ray into the darkness. But if any such had existed in the background of Boyne's life, they had disappeared as completely as the slip of paper on which the visitor had written his name. There remained no possible thread of guidance except -- if it were indeed an exception -- the letter which Boyne had apparently been in the act of writing when he received his mysterious summons. That letter, read and reread by his wife, and submitted by her to the police, yielded little enough for conjecture to feed on.

"I have just heard of Elwell's death, and while I suppose there is now no farther risk of trouble, it might be safer --" That was all. The "risk of trouble" was easily explained by the newspaper clipping which had apprised Mary of the suit brought against her husband by one of his associates in the Blue Star enterprise. The only new information conveyed in the letter was the fact of its showing Boyne, when he wrote it, to be still apprehensive of the results of the suit, though he had assured his wife that it had been withdrawn, and though the letter itself declared that the plaintiff was dead. It took several weeks of exhaustive cabling to fix the identity of the "Parvis" to whom the fragmentary communication was addressed, but even after these inquiries had shown him to be a Waukesha lawyer, no new facts concerning the Elwell suit were elicited. He appeared to have had no direct concern in it, but to have been conversant with the facts merely as an acquaintance, and possible intermediary; and he declared himself unable to divine with what object Boyne intended to seek his assistance.

This negative information, sole fruit of the first fortnight's feverish search, was not increased by a jot during the slow weeks that followed. Mary knew that the investigations were still being carried on, but she had a vague sense of their gradually slackening, as the actual march of time seemed to slacken. It was as though the days, flying horror-struck from the shrouded image of the one inscrutable day, gained assurance as the distance lengthened, till at last they fell back into their normal gait. And so with the human imaginations at work on the dark event. No doubt it occupied them still, but week by week and hour by hour it grew less absorbing, took up less space, was slowly but inevitably crowded out of the foreground of consciousness by the new problems perpetually bubbling up from the vaporous caldron of human experience.

Even Mary Boyne's consciousness gradually felt the same lowering of velocity. It still swayed with the incessant oscillations of conjecture; but they were slower, more rhythmical in their beat. There were moments of overwhelming lassitude when, like the victim of some poison which leaves the brain clear, but holds the body motionless, she saw herself domesticated with the Horror, accepting its perpetual presence as one of the fixed conditions of life.

These moments lengthened into hours and days, till she passed into a phase of stolid acquiescence. She watched the familiar routine of life with the incurious eye of a savage on whom the meaningless processes of civilization make but the faintest impression. She had come to regard herself as part of the routine, a spoke of the wheel, revolving with its motion; she felt almost like the furniture of the room in which she sat, an insensate object to be dusted and pushed about with the chairs and tables. And this deepening apathy held her fast at Lyng, in spite of the urgent entreaties of friends and the usual medical recommendation of "change." Her friends supposed that her refusal to move was inspired by the belief that her husband would one day return to the spot from which he had vanished, and a beautiful legend grew up about this imaginary state of waiting. But in reality she had no such belief: the depths of anguish inclosing her were no longer lighted by flashes of hope. She was sure that Boyne would never come back, that he had gone out of her sight as completely as if Death itself had waited that day on the threshold. She had even renounced, one by one, the various theories as to his disappearance which had been advanced by the press, the police, and her own agonized imagination. In sheer lassitude her mind turned from these alternatives of horror, and sank back into the blank fact that he was gone.

No, she would never know what had become of him -- no one would ever know. But the house knew; the library in which she spent her long, lonely evenings knew. For it was here that the last scene had been enacted, here that the stranger had come, and spoken the word which had caused Boyne to rise and follow him. The floor she trod had felt his tread; the books on the shelves had seen his face; and there were moments when the intense consciousness of the old, dusky walls seemed about to break out into some audible revelation of their secret. But the revelation never came, and she knew it would never come. Lyng was not one of the garrulous old houses that betray the secrets intrusted to them. Its very legend proved that it had always been the mute accomplice, the incorruptible custodian of the mysteries it had surprised. And Mary Boyne, sitting face to face with its portentous silence, felt the futility of seeking to break it by any human means.

V

"I don't say it wasn't straight, yet don't say it was straight. It was business."

Mary, at the words, lifted her head with a start, and looked intently at the speaker.

When, half an hour before, a card with "Mr. Parvis" on it had been brought up to her, she had been immediately aware that the name had been a part of her consciousness ever since she had read it at the head of Boyne's unfinished letter. In the library she had found awaiting her a small neutral-tinted man with a bald head and gold eye-glasses, and it sent a strange tremor through her to know that this was the person to whom her husband's last known thought had been directed.

Parvis, civilly, but without vain preamble, -- in the manner of a man who has his watch in his hand, -- had set forth the object of his visit. He had "run over" to England on business, and finding himself in the neighborhood of Dorchester, had not wished to leave it without paying his respects to Mrs. Boyne; without asking her, if the occasion offered, what she meant to do about Bob Elwell's family.

The words touched the spring of some obscure dread in Mary's bosom. Did her visitor, after all, know what Boyne had meant by his unfinished phrase? She asked for an elucidation of his question, and noticed at once that he seemed surprised at her continued ignorance of the subject. Was it possible that she really knew as little as she said?

"I know nothing -- you must tell me," she faltered out;

and her visitor thereupon proceeded to unfold his story. It threw, even to her confused perceptions, and imperfectly initiated vision, a lurid glare on the whole hazy episode of the Blue Star Mine. Her husband had made his money in that brilliant speculation at the cost of "getting ahead" of some one less alert to seize the chance; the victim of his ingenuity was young Robert Elwell, who had "put him on" to the Blue Star scheme.

Parvis, at Mary's first startled cry, had thrown her a sobering glance through his impartial glasses.

"Bob Elwell wasn't smart enough, that's all; if he had been, he might have turned round and served Boyne the same way. It's the kind of thing that happens every day in business. I guess it's what the scientists call the survival of the fittest," said Mr. Parvis, evidently pleased with the aptness of his analogy.

Mary felt a physical shrinking from the next question she tried to frame; it was as though the words on her lips had a taste that nauseated her.

"But then -- you accuse my husband of doing something dishonorable?"

Mr. Parvis surveyed the question dispassionately. "Oh, no, I don't. I don't even say it wasn't straight." He glanced up and down the long lines of books, as if one of them might have supplied him with the definition he sought. "I don't say it wasn't straight, and yet I don't say it was straight. It was business." After all, no definition in his category could be more comprehensive than that.

Mary sat staring at him with a look of terror. He seemed to her like the indifferent, implacable emissary of some dark, formless power.

"But Mr. Elwell's lawyers apparently did not take your view, since I suppose the suit was withdrawn by their advice."

"Oh, yes, they knew he hadn't a leg to stand on, technically. It was when they advised him to withdraw the suit that he got desperate. You see, he'd borrowed most of the money he lost in the Blue Star, and he was up a tree. That's why he shot himself when they told him he had no show."

The horror was sweeping over Mary in great, deafening waves.

"He shot himself? He killed himself because of that? "

"Well, he didn't kill himself, exactly. He dragged on two months before he died." Parvis emitted the statement as unemotionally as a gramophone grinding out its "record."

"You mean that he tried to kill himself, and failed? And tried again?"

"Oh, he didn't have to try again," said Parvis, grimly.

They sat opposite each other in silence, he swinging his eyeglass thoughtfully about his finger, she, motionless, her arms stretched along her knees in an attitude of rigid tension.

"But if you knew all this," she began at length, hardly able to force her voice above a whisper, "how is it that when I wrote you at the time of my husband's disappearance you said you didn't understand his letter?"

Parvis received this without perceptible discomfiture. "Why, I didn't understand it -- strictly speaking. And it wasn't the time to talk about it, if I had. The Elwell business was settled when the suit was withdrawn. Nothing I could have told you would have helped you to find your husband."

Mary continued to scrutinize him. "Then why are you telling me now?"

Still Parvis did not hesitate. "Well, to begin with, I supposed you knew more than you appear to -- I mean about the circumstances of Elwell's death. And then people are talking of it now; the whole matter's been raked up again. And I thought, if you didn't know, you ought to."

She remained silent, and he continued: "You see, it's only come out lately what a bad state Elwell's affairs were in. His wife's a proud woman, and she fought on as long as she could, going out to work, and taking sewing at home, when she got too sick-something with the heart, I believe. But she had his bedridden mother to look after, and the children, and she broke down under it, and finally had to ask for help. That attracted attention to the case, and the papers took it up, and a subscription was started. Everybody out there liked Bob Elwell, and most of the prominent names in the place are down on the list, and people began to wonder why --"

Parvis broke off to fumble in an inner pocket. "Here," he continued, "here's an account of the whole thing from the 'Sentinel' -- a little sensational, of course. But I guess you'd better look it over."

He held out a newspaper to Mary, who unfolded it slowly, remembering, as she did so, the evening when, in that same room, the perusal of a clipping from the "Sentinel" had first shaken the depths of her security.

As she opened the paper, her eyes, shrinking from the glaring head-lines, "Widow of Boyne's Victim Forced to Appeal for Aid," ran down the column of text to two portraits inserted in it. The first was her husband's, taken from a photograph made the year they had come to England. It was the picture of him that she liked best, the one that stood on the writing-table up-stairs in her bedroom. As the eyes in the photograph met hers, she felt it would be impossible to read what was said of him, and closed her lids with the sharpness of the pain.

"I thought if you felt disposed to put your name down --" she heard Parvis continue.

She opened her eyes with an effort, and they fell on the other portrait. It was that of a youngish man, slightly built, in rough clothes, with features somewhat blurred by the shadow of a projecting hat-brim. Where had she seen that outline before? She stared at it confusedly, her heart hammering in her throat and ears. Then she gave a cry.

"This is the man -- the man who came for my husband!"

She heard Parvis start to his feet, and was dimly aware that she had slipped backward into the corner of the sofa, and that he was bending above her in alarm. With an intense effort she straightened herself, and reached out for the paper, which she had dropped.

"It's the man! I should know him anywhere!" she cried in a voice that sounded in her own ears like a scream.

Parvis's voice seemed to come to her from far off, down endless, fog-muffled windings.

"Mrs. Boyne, you're not very well. Shall I call somebody? Shall I get a glass of water?"

"No, no, no!" She threw herself toward him, her hand frantically clenching the newspaper. "I tell you, it's the man! I know him! He spoke to me in the garden!"

Parvis took the journal from her, directing his glasses to the portrait. "It can't be, Mrs. Boyne. It's Robert Elwell."

"Robert Elwell?" Her white stare seemed to travel into space. "Then it was Robert Elwell who came for him."

"Came for Boyne? The day he went away?" Parvis's voice dropped as hers rose. He bent over, laying a fraternal hand on her, as if to coax her gently back into her seat. "Why, Elwell was dead! Don't you remember?"

Mary sat with her eyes fixed on the picture, unconscious of what he was saying.

"Don't you remember Boyne's unfinished letter to me -- the one you found on his desk that day? It was written just after he'd heard of Elwell's death." She noticed an odd shake in Parvis's unemotional voice. "Surely you remember that!" he urged her.

Yes, she remembered: that was the profoundest horror of it. Elwell had died the day before her husband's disappearance; and this was Elwell's portrait; and it was the portrait of the man who had spoken to her in the garden. She lifted her head and looked slowly about the library. The library could have borne witness that it was also the portrait of the man who had come in that day to call Boyne from his unfinished letter. Through the misty surgings of her brain she heard the faint boom of halfforgotten words -- words spoken by Alida Stair on the lawn at Pangbourne before Boyne and his wife had ever seen the house at Lyng, or had imagined that they might one day live there..

"This was the man who spoke to me," she repeated.

She looked again at Parvis. He was trying to conceal his disturbance under what he imagined to be an expression of indulgent commiseration; but the edges of his lips were blue. "He thinks me mad; but I'm not mad," she reflected; and suddenly there flashed upon her a way of justifying her strange affirmation.

She sat quiet, controlling the quiver of her lips, and waiting till she could trust her voice to keep its habitual level; then she said, looking straight at Parvis: "Will you answer me one question, please? When was it that Robert Elwell tried to kill himself?"

"When -- when?" Parvis stammered.

"Yes; the date. Please try to remember."

She saw that he was growing still more afraid of her. "I have a reason," she insisted gently.

"Yes, yes. Only I can't remember. About two months before, I should say."

"I want the date," she repeated.

Parvis picked up the newspaper. "We might see here," he said, still humoring her. He ran his eyes down the page. "Here it is. Last October -- the --"

She caught the words from him. "The 20th, wasn't it?" With a sharp look at her, he verified. "Yes, the 20th. Then you did know?"

"I know now." Her white stare continued to travel past him. "Sunday, the 20th -- that was the day he came first."

Parvis's voice was almost inaudible. "Came here first?"

"Yes."

"You saw him twice, then?"

"Yes, twice." She breathed it at him with dilated eyes. "He came first on the 20th of October. I remember the date because it was the day we went up Meldon Steep for the first time." She felt a faint gasp of inward laughter at the thought that but for that she might have forgotten.

Parvis continued to scrutinize her, as if trying to intercept her gaze.

"We saw him from the roof," she went on. "He came down the limeavenue toward the house. He was dressed just as he is in that picture. My husband saw him first. He was frightened, and ran down ahead of me; but there was no one there. He had vanished."

"Elwell had vanished?" Parvis faltered.

"Yes." Their two whispers seemed to grope for each other. "I couldn't think what had happened. I see now. He tried to come then; but he wasn't dead enough -- he couldn't reach us. He had to wait for two months; and then he came back again -- and Ned went with him."

She nodded at Parvis with the look of triumph of a child who has successfully worked out a difficult puzzle. But suddenly she lifted her hands with a desperate gesture, pressing them to her bursting temples.

"Oh, my God! I sent him to Ned -- I told him where to go! I sent him to this room!" she screamed out.

She felt the walls of the room rush toward her, like inward falling ruins; and she heard Parvis, a long way off, as if through the ruins, crying to her, and struggling to get at her. But she was numb to his touch, she did not know what he was saying. Through the tumult she heard but one clear note, the voice of Alida Stair, speaking on the lawn at Pangbourne.

"You won't know till afterward," it said. "You won't know till long, long afterward."

A Journey

As she lay in her berth, staring at the shadows overhead, the rush of the wheels was in her brain, driving her deeper and deeper into circles of wakeful lucidity. The sleeping-car had sunk into its night-silence. Through the wet window-pane she watched the sudden lights, the long stretches of hurrying blackness. Now and then she turned her head and looked through the opening in the hangings at her husband's curtains across the aisle....

She wondered restlessly if he wanted anything and if she could hear him if he called. His voice had grown very weak within the last months and it irritated him when she did not hear. This irritability, this increasing childish petulance seemed to give expression to their imperceptible estrangement. Like two faces looking at one another through a sheet of glass they were close together, almost touching, but they could not hear or feel each other: the conductivity between them was broken. She, at least, had this sense of separation, and she fancied sometimes that she saw it reflected in the look with which he supplemented his failing words. Doubtless the fault was hers. She was too impenetrably healthy to be touched by the irrelevancies of disease. Her self-reproachful tenderness was tinged with the sense of his irrationality: she had a vague feeling that there was a purpose in his helpless tyrannies. The suddenness of the change had found her so unprepared. A year ago their pulses had beat to one robust measure; both had the same prodigal confidence in an exhaustless future. Now their energies no longer kept step: hers still bounded ahead of life, preempting unclaimed regions of hope and activity, while his lagged behind, vainly struggling to overtake her.

When they married, she had such arrears of living to make up: her days had been as bare as the whitewashed school-room where she forced innutritious facts upon reluctant children. His coming had broken in on the slumber of circumstance, widening the present till it became the encloser of remotest chances. But imperceptibly the horizon narrowed. Life had a grudge against her: she was never to be allowed to spread her wings.

At first the doctors had said that six weeks of mild air would set him right; but when he came back this assurance was explained as having of course included a winter in a dry climate. They gave up their pretty house, storing the wedding presents and new furniture, and went to Colorado. She had hated it there from the first. Nobody knew her or cared about her; there was no one to wonder at the good match she had made, or to envy her the new dresses and the visiting-cards which were still a surprise to her. And he kept growing worse. She felt herself beset with difficulties too evasive to be fought by so direct a temperament. She still loved him, of course; but he was gradually, undefinably ceasing to be himself. The man she had married had been strong, active, gently masterful: the male whose pleasure it is to clear a way through the material obstructions of life; but now it was she who was the protector, he who must be shielded from importunities and given his drops or his beef-juice though the skies were falling. The routine of the sick-room bewildered her; this punctual administering of medicine seemed as idle as some uncomprehended religious mummery.

There were moments, indeed, when warm gushes of pity swept away her instinctive resentment of his condition, when she still found his old self in his eyes as they groped for each other through the dense medium of his weakness. But these moments had grown rare. Sometimes he frightened her: his sunken expressionless face seemed that of a stranger; his voice was weak and hoarse; his thin-lipped smile a mere muscular contraction. Her hand avoided his damp soft skin, which had lost the familiar roughness of health: she caught herself furtively watching him as she might have watched a strange animal. It frightened her to feel that this was the man she loved; there were hours when to tell him what she suffered seemed the one escape from her fears. But in general she judged herself more leniently, reflecting that she had perhaps been too long alone with him, and that she would feel differently when they were at home again, surrounded by her robust and buoyant family. How she had rejoiced when the doctors at last gave their consent to his going home! She knew, of course, what the decision meant; they both knew. It meant that he was to die; but they dressed the truth in hopeful euphuisms, and at times, in the joy of preparation, she really forgot the purpose of their journey, and slipped into an eager allusion to next year's plans.

At last the day of leaving came. She had a dreadful fear that they would never get away; that somehow at the last moment he would fail her; that the doctors held one of their accustomed treacheries in reserve; but nothing happened.

They drove to the station, he was installed in a seat with a rug over his knees and a cushion at his back, and she hung out of the window waving unregretful farewells to the acquaintances she had really never liked till then.

The first twenty-four hours had passed off well. He revived a little and it amused him to look out of the window and to observe the humours of the car. The second day he began to grow weary and to chafe under the dispassionate stare of the freckled child with the lump of chewing-gum. She had to explain to the child's mother that her husband was too ill to be disturbed: a statement received by that lady with a resentment visibly supported by the maternal sentiment of the whole car....

That night he slept badly and the next morning his temperature frightened her: she was sure he was growing worse. The day passed slowly, punctuated by the small irritations of travel. Watching his tired face, she traced in its contractions every rattle and jolt of the tram, till her own body vibrated with sympathetic fatigue. She felt the others observing him too, and hovered restlessly between him and the line of interrogative eyes. The freckled child hung about him like a fly; offers of candy and picture- books failed to dislodge her: she twisted one leg around the other and watched him imperturbably. The porter, as he passed, lingered with vague proffers of help, probably inspired by philanthropic passengers swelling with the sense that "something ought to be done;" and one nervous man in a skull-cap was audibly concerned as to the possible effect on his wife's health.

The hours dragged on in a dreary inoccupation. Towards dusk she sat down beside him and he laid his hand on hers.

The touch startled her. He seemed to be calling her from far off. She looked at him helplessly and his smile went through her like a physical pang.

"Are you very tired?" she asked.

"No, not very."

"We'll be there soon now."

"Yes, very soon."

"This time to-morrow -"

He nodded and they sat silent. When she had put him to bed and crawled into her own berth she tried to cheer herself with the thought that in less than twenty-four hours they would be in New York. Her people would all be at the station to meet her--she pictured their round unanxious faces pressing through the crowd. She only hoped they would not tell him too loudly that he was looking splendidly and would be all right in no time: the subtler sympathies developed by long contact with suffering were making her aware of a certain coarseness of texture in the family sensibilities.

Suddenly she thought she heard him call. She parted the curtains and listened. No, it was only a man snoring at the other end of the car. His snores had a greasy sound, as though they passed through tallow. She lay down and tried to sleep... Had she not heard him move? She started up trembling... The silence frightened her more than any sound. He might not be able to make her hear--he might be calling her now... What made her think of such things?

It was merely the familiar tendency of an over-tired mind to fasten itself on the most intolerable chance within the range of its forebodings.... Putting her head out, she listened; but she could not distinguish his breathing from that of the other pairs of lungs about her. She longed to get up and look at him, but she knew the impulse was a mere vent for her restlessness, and the fear of disturbing him restrained her.... The regular movement of his curtain reassured her, she knew not why; she remembered that he had wished her a cheerful good-night; and the sheer inability to endure her fears a moment longer made her put them from her with an effort of her whole sound tired body. She turned on her side and slept.

She sat up stiffly, staring out at the dawn. The train was rushing through a region of bare hillocks huddled against a lifeless sky. It looked like the first day of creation. The air of the car was close, and she pushed up her window to let in the keen wind. Then she looked at her watch: it was seven o'clock, and soon the people about her would be stirring. She slipped into her clothes, smoothed her dishevelled hair and crept to the dressing-room. When she had washed her face and adjusted her dress she felt more hopeful. It was always a struggle for her not to be cheerful in the morning. Her cheeks burned deliciously under the coarse towel and the wet hair about her temples broke into strong upward tendrils. Every inch of her was full of life and elasticity. And in ten hours they would be at home!

She stepped to her husband's berth: it was time for him to take his early glass of milk. The window-shade was down, and in the dusk of the curtained enclosure she could just see that he lay sideways, with his face away from her. She leaned over him and drew up the shade. As she did so she touched one of his hands. It felt cold....

She bent closer, laying her hand on his arm and calling him by name. He did not move. She spoke again more loudly; she grasped his shoulder and gently shook it. He lay motionless. She caught hold of his hand again: it slipped from her limply, like a dead thing. A dead thing? ... Her breath caught. She must see his face. She leaned forward, and hurriedly, shrinkingly, with a sickening reluctance of the flesh, laid her hands on his shoulders and turned him over. His head fell back; his face looked small and smooth; he gazed at her with steady eyes.

She remained motionless for a long time, holding him thus; and they looked at each other. Suddenly she shrank back: the longing to scream, to call out, to fly from him, had almost overpowered her. But a strong hand arrested her. Good God! If it were known that he was dead they would be put off the train at the next station--

In a terrifying flash of remembrance there arose before her a scene she had once witnessed in travelling, when a husband and wife, whose child had died in the train, had been thrust out at some chance station. She saw them standing on the platform with the child's body between them; she had never forgotten the dazed look with which they followed the receding train. And this was what would happen to her. Within the next hour she might find herself on the platform of some strange station, alone with her husband's body.... Anything but that! It was too horrible--She quivered like a creature at bay.

As she cowered there, she felt the train moving more

slowly. It was coming then--they were approaching a station! She saw again the husband and wife standing on the lonely platform; and with a violent gesture she drew down the shade to hide her husband's face.

Feeling dizzy, she sank down on the edge of the berth, keeping away from his outstretched body, and pulling the curtains close, so that he and she were shut into a kind of sepulchral twilight. She tried to think. At all costs she must conceal the fact that he was dead. But how? Her mind refused to act: she could not plan, combine. She could think of no way but to sit there, clutching the curtains, all day long....

She heard the porter making up her bed; people were beginning to move about the car; the dressing-room door was being opened and shut. She tried to rouse herself. At length with a supreme effort she rose to her feet, stepping into the aisle of the car and drawing the curtains tight behind her. She noticed that they still parted slightly with the motion of the car, and finding a pin in her dress she fastened them together. Now she was safe. She looked round and saw the porter. She fancied he was watching her.

"Ain't he awake yet?" he enquired.

"No," she faltered.

"I got his milk all ready when he wants it. You know you told me to have it for him by seven."

She nodded silently and crept into her seat.

At half-past eight the train reached Buffalo. By this time

the other passengers were dressed and the berths had been folded back for the day. The porter, moving to and fro under his burden of sheets and pillows, glanced at her as he passed. At length he said: "Ain't he going to get up? You know we're ordered to make up the berths as early as we can."

She turned cold with fear. They were just entering the station.

"Oh, not yet," she stammered. "Not till he's had his milk. Won't you get it, please?"

"All right. Soon as we start again."

When the train moved on he reappeared with the milk. She took it from him and sat vaguely looking at it: her brain moved slowly from one idea to another, as though they were stepping-stones set far apart across a whirling flood. At length she became aware that the porter still hovered expectantly.

"Will I give it to him?" he suggested.

"Oh, no," she cried, rising. "He--he's asleep yet, I think--"

She waited till the porter had passed on; then she unpinned the curtains and slipped behind them. In the semi-obscurity her husband's face stared up at her like a marble mask with agate eyes. The eyes were dreadful. She put out her hand and drew down the lids. Then she remembered the glass of milk in her other hand: what was she to do with it? She thought of raising the window and throwing it out; but to do so she would have to lean across his body and bring her face close to his. She decided to drink the milk.

She returned to her seat with the empty glass and after a while the porter came back to get it.

"When'll I fold up his bed?" he asked.

"Oh, not now--not yet; he's ill--he's very ill. Can't you let him stay as he is? The doctor wants him to lie down as much as possible."

He scratched his head. "Well, if he's _really_ sick--"

He took the empty glass and walked away, explaining to the passengers that the party behind the curtains was too sick to get up just yet.

She found herself the centre of sympathetic eyes. A motherly woman with an intimate smile sat down beside her.

"I'm real sorry to hear your husband's sick. I've had a remarkable amount of sickness in my family and maybe I could assist you. Can I take a look at him?"

"Oh, no--no, please! He mustn't be disturbed."

The lady accepted the rebuff indulgently.

"Well, it's just as you say, of course, but you don't look to me as if you'd had much experience in sickness and I'd have been glad to assist you. What do you generally do when your husband's taken this way?"

"I--I let him sleep."

"Too much sleep ain't any too healthful either. Don't you give him any medicine?"

"Y--yes."

"Don't you wake him to take it?"

"Yes."

"When does he take the next dose?"

"Not for--two hours--"

The lady looked disappointed. "Well, if I was you I'd try giving it oftener. That's what I do with my folks."

After that many faces seemed to press upon her. The passengers were on their way to the dining-car, and she was conscious that as they passed down the aisle they glanced curiously at the closed curtains. One lantern- jawed man with prominent eyes stood still and tried to shoot his projecting glance through the division between the folds. The freckled child, returning from breakfast, waylaid the passers with a buttery clutch, saying in a loud whisper, "He's sick;" and once the conductor came by, asking for tickets. She shrank into her corner and looked out of the window at the flying trees and houses, meaningless hieroglyphs of an endlessly unrolled papyrus.

Now and then the train stopped, and the newcomers on entering the car stared in turn at the closed curtains. More and more people seemed to pass--their faces began to blend fantastically with the images surging in her brain....

Later in the day a fat man detached himself from the mist of faces. He had a creased stomach and soft pale lips. As he pressed himself into the seat facing her she noticed that he was dressed in black broadcloth, with a soiled white tie.

"Husband's pretty bad this morning, is he?"

"Yes."

"Dear, dear! Now that's terribly distressing, ain't it?" An apostolic smile revealed his gold-filled teeth.

"Of course you know there's no sech thing as sickness. Ain't that a lovely thought? Death itself is but a deloosion of our grosser senses. On'y lay yourself open to the influx of the sperrit, submit yourself passively to the action of the divine force, and disease and dissolution will cease to exist for you. If you could indooce your husband to read this little pamphlet--"

The faces about her again grew indistinct. She had a vague recollection of hearing the motherly lady and the parent of the freckled child ardently disputing the relative advantages of trying several medicines at once, or of taking each in turn; the motherly lady maintaining that the competitive system saved time; the other objecting that you couldn't tell which remedy had effected the cure; their voices went on and on, like bell-buoys droning through a fog.... The porter came up now and then with questions that she did not understand, but that somehow she must have answered since he went away again without repeating them; every two hours the motherly lady reminded her that her husband ought to have his drops; people left the car and others replaced them...

Her head was spinning and she tried to steady herself by clutching at her thoughts as they swept by, but they slipped away from her like bushes on the side of a sheer precipice down which she seemed to be falling. Suddenly her mind grew clear again and she found herself vividly picturing what would happen when the train reached New York. She shuddered as it occurred to her that he would be quite cold and that some one might perceive he had been dead since morning.

She thought hurriedly:--"If they see I am not surprised they will suspect something. They will ask questions, and if I tell them the truth they won't believe me--no one would believe me! It will be terrible"--and she kept repeating to herself:--"I must pretend I don't know. I must pretend I don't know. When they open the curtains I must go up to him quite naturally--and then I must scream." ... She had an idea that the scream would be very hard to do.

Gradually new thoughts crowded upon her, vivid and urgent: she tried to separate and restrain them, but they beset her clamorously, like her school-children at the end of a hot day, when she was too tired to silence them. Her head grew confused, and she felt a sick fear of forgetting her part, of betraying herself by some unguarded word or look.

"I must pretend I don't know," she went on murmuring. The words had lost their significance, but she repeated them mechanically, as though they had been a magic formula, until suddenly she heard herself saying: "I can't remember, I can't remember!"

Her voice sounded very loud, and she looked about her in terror; but no one seemed to notice that she had spoken.

As she glanced down the car her eye caught the curtains of her husband's berth, and she began to examine the monotonous arabesques woven through their heavy folds. The pattern was intricate and difficult to trace; she gazed fixedly at the curtains and as she did so the thick stuff grew transparent and through it she saw her husband's face--his dead face. She struggled to avert her look, but her eyes refused to move and her head seemed to be held in a vice. At last, with an effort that left her weak and shaking, she turned away; but it was of no use; close in front of her, small and smooth, was her husband's face. It seemed to be suspended in the air between her and the false braids of the woman who sat in front of her. With an uncontrollable gesture she stretched out her hand to push the face away, and suddenly she felt the touch of his smooth skin. She repressed a cry and half started from her seat. The woman with the false braids looked around, and feeling that she must justify her movement in some way she rose and lifted her travelling-bag from the opposite seat. She unlocked the bag and looked into it; but the first object her hand met was a small flask of her husband's, thrust there at the last moment, in the haste of departure. She locked the bag and closed her eyes ... his face was there again, hanging between her eye-balls and lids like a waxen mask against a red curtain....

She roused herself with a shiver. Had she fainted or slept? Hours seemed to have elapsed; but it was still broad day, and the people about her were sitting in the same attitudes as before.

A sudden sense of hunger made her aware that she had eaten nothing since morning. The thought of food filled her with disgust, but she dreaded a return of faintness, and remembering that she had some biscuits in her bag she took one out and ate it. The dry crumbs choked her, and she hastily swallowed a little brandy from her husband's flask. The burning sensation in her throat acted as a counter-irritant, momentarily relieving the dull ache of her nerves. Then she felt a gently-stealing warmth, as though a soft air fanned her, and the swarming fears relaxed their clutch, receding through the stillness that enclosed her, a stillness soothing as the spacious quietude of a summer day. She slept.

Through her sleep she felt the impetuous rush of the train. It seemed to be life itself that was sweeping her on with headlong inexorable force-- sweeping her into darkness and terror, and the awe of unknown days.--Now all at once everything was still--not a sound, not a pulsation... She was dead in her turn, and lay beside him with smooth upstaring face. How quiet it was!--and yet she heard feet coming, the feet of the men who were to carry them away... She could feel too--she felt a sudden prolonged vibration, a series of hard shocks, and then another plunge into darkness: the darkness of death this time--a black whirlwind on which they were both spinning like leaves, in wild uncoiling spirals, with millions and millions of the dead....

* * *

She sprang up in terror. Her sleep must have lasted a long time, for the winter day had paled and the lights had been lit. The car was in confusion, and as she regained her self-possession she saw that the passengers were gathering up their wraps and bags. The woman with the false braids had brought from the dressing-room a sickly ivy-plant in a bottle, and the Christian Scientist was reversing his cuffs.

The porter passed down the aisle with his impartial brush. An impersonal figure with a gold-banded cap asked for her husband's ticket. A voice shouted "Baig- gage express!" and she heard the clicking of metal as the passengers handed over their checks.

Presently her window was blocked by an expanse of sooty wall, and the train passed into the Harlem tunnel. The journey was over; in a few minutes she would see her family pushing their joyous way through the throng at the station. Her heart dilated. The worst terror was past....

"We'd better get him up now, hadn't we?" asked the porter, touching her arm.

He had her husband's hat in his hand and was meditatively revolving it under his brush.

She looked at the hat and tried to speak; but suddenly the car grew dark. She flung up her arms, struggling to catch at something, and fell face downward, striking her head against the dead man's berth.

Short Stories Library
Other authors in the Collection

Herman Melville
Kate Chopin
Susan Glaspell
Harriet Beecher Stowe
Mark Twain
Edgar Allan Poe
Oscar Wilde
Hans Christian Andersen
H.G. Wells
Ernest Hemingway
Nathaniel Hawthorne
Anton Chekhov
Rudyard Kipling
Louisa May Alcott
Virginia Woolf
Mary Shelley
Mary E. Wilkins Freeman
Elia W. Peattie
Amelia B. Edwards
Evelyn Everett-Green
T.S. Arthur
Alice Dunbar-Nelson
Sarah Orne Jewett
Katherine Mansfield
Mary Hallock Foote
Laura E. Richards
Charlotte M. Yonge
Willa Cather
Sarah Orne Jewett
Mary Roberts Rinehart
Lucy Maud Montgomery

TBC...

Printed in Great Britain
by Amazon